Father Confessor

A **J McNee** Novel

Russel D McLean

Five Leaves Publications

www.fiveleaves.co.uk

Father Confessor
by Russel D McLean

Published in 2012 by Five Leaves Publications,
PO Box 8786, Nottingham NG1 9AW
www.fiveleaves.co.uk

ISBN: 9781907869549

Five Leaves acknowledges support
from Arts Council England

Five Leaves is represented to the trade
by Turnaround and distributed by Central Books

Typeset, design and cover design by
Four Sheets Design and Print

Printed and bound in Great Britain
by Russell Press, Nottingham

I wasn't there.

If I had been, things might have turned out different.

I'd like to believe that.

Some would argue, of course, that I'd only have fucked things up.

For months afterward, I would spend the hours past midnight – the hours when I couldn't sleep, when the guilt of the past always seemed at its strongest and when I felt at my most powerless and insignificant – thinking about what had happened that evening.

Seeing events through his eyes.

Trying to imagine what it must have been like. Trying to think about the chain of events that ended in a moment of blood and fear and pain.

As I tried to imagine how he felt, my heart would pound as his must have. A surge of adrenaline. An expectation.

He must have known that he was going to die.

One way or the other. He must have known how things would end.

Maybe he had come to terms with that idea.

Looking back over his last few months, talking to friends and colleagues, I think they all knew that something was wrong with him. They had sensed his growing unease. They had noticed that he was more tense than usual. Most put this down to pre-retirement nerves. After all, he was due to quit the force in the next year. And like any good copper, he had a lot of unfinished business.

So I can imagine how he felt that night.

Walking into the warehouse, he might have called out. Perhaps listened to the echo of his own voice, heard it come back to him. A ghost-like echo. As though he was already dead. His own footsteps – polished shoes striking hard concrete – would have bounced and echoed around the wide space and made it appear as though there were others walking alongside him.

Those for whom he was responsible.

Maybe he was thinking about why he was here. The reasons he was alone in this warehouse, meeting a man he must have known could kill him.

He would be thinking about his career. And his daughter.

His daughter who was under investigation for possible criminal conspiracy. His daughter who had always been the centre of his world, who had idolised her father so much she followed him into the force.

I would wonder what he was thinking.

How he felt.

And I could never know for sure. But I had to pretend, to try and gain some insight the hard facts could never uncover.

I do know that he took the stairs to the mezzanine slowly. His shoes clanking off the metal grille, his hand running up the banister. A feather touch. More for reassurance than balance.

But then, maybe his grip was tighter than usual. He was afraid of falling away. Of losing his grip.

Maybe he came knowing that he faced death.

He would do that on his own terms.

The idea makes me feel better in a way.

There had been no signs of a struggle when the coppers arrived on the scene. He did not fight back. He did not try to run.

On the metal walkway high above the main floor, he would have been confronted by the man with the shotgun.

Did they speak?

Did he understand why the man was there to kill him?

I don't know. I wasn't there.

And I wish I had been.

Some nights I wish it had been me and not him.

The impact of the shot knocked him over the safety rails. Did he have time to register what was happening?

Did he say a prayer as he fell?

I wonder about his final thoughts. What he saw. What was revealed to him as he lay crooked on the floor of the abandoned mill, his blood pooling around his head, his limbs twisted.

Did he think of his killer?

Of his daughter?

I would have been the furthest thing from his mind. But if he felt a small twinge of disappointment, perhaps he was remembering me and the last time we spoke, the things I said to him.

But I don't know any of that.

I just believe that I could sleep easier if I knew what he was really thinking in those last moments.

ONE

DI George Lindsay stood in the close. Unshaven. Suit and shirt wrinkled. Bags under his eyes. His high forehead jutted, tiny eyes glaring out malevolently from underneath.

He said, "I need to talk to your girlfriend."

Complete sentence. No swear words. Whatever he was here to talk about, it was important.

I said, "She isn't here." All bravado, but my heart was jacking in my chest. Nausea kept rising in waves and I had to fight to keep from puking all over the DI's shoes. Not that it would have made much difference to his image that morning.

Call it guilt.

The fear of being caught in a lie.

We'd been waiting months for an official decision. It couldn't come like this. But then, as I knew, life has a way of knocking you on your arse when you least expect it.

Lindsay said, "It's official business."

Was this it, then?

Susan had been under investigation since covering up a murder nearly sixteen months earlier. She took the rap for a killing that would otherwise have implicated a terrified fifteen-year-old girl. She did this to protect the girl.

And me.

That was the worst part. We'd agreed that Mary Furst hadn't been in her right mind when she thrust an axe into the spine of the man who had, ten minutes earlier, beaten her mother's skull open. We'd agreed that I would take the blame, claim it as a case of self-defence.

And then Susan stepped forward, claimed she was the one who killed the man we knew only as Wickes.

Putting herself on the line. Personally and professionally.

I said, "Is she being formally charged?"

Lindsay shook his head. "Fuck that," he said. He had been her partner in the CID during her first year as a DS. He cared for her in his way. I don't think he wanted the investigation to uncover any wrongdoing on Susan's part. All the same, he held anyone in the job to high standards, and I thought that if she was found guilty, he'd be the first to turn his back.

As a matter of pride.

"It's her dad. Ernie. The poor bugger's been murdered."

#

I knew where to find Susan.

Didn't tell Lindsay that, of course. Figuring the burden lay with me. It seemed right that I should tell her.

Nothing to do with the antagonism between me and a certain DI who could have been mistaken for a missing link in the wrong light. Or even the right light.

I drove to Riverside. Walked east along the curve of the river with the dark water silent on one side and the rush of cars along the dual carriageway on the other.

Found her taking a breather, leaning on the stone dyke that stood between the unwary pedestrian and a watery grave. There was a light sheen of sweat on her forehead. She was flushed from the run, grinning from the adrenaline high.

Susan sucked down water from a plastic bottle, nodded as I approached. It was a cool day, the skies overcast, but she was still sweating, soaked through her grey cotton T-shirt.

She said, "You're not out for the exercise." Gave me a grin. The kind of grin that said she knew something was wrong, didn't want it to intrude.

I like to think I have what they call a poker face. It never works with Susan. She's one of only two people who've ever been able to read me.

I leaned on the stone beside her, facing out to the river. She mirrored me. Neither of us looked at the other. Just at the splintered reflection of the early morning sky in the water.

I said, "You need to call Lindsay."

"You forget I'm suspended. He can't even ask me for help wiping his nose."

"It's not about the investigation."

When I'd been a copper, the job I hated most was delivering bad news to families, loved ones, friends. Telling someone that a person they'd known for years was dead used to get passed out amongst attending officers like a lottery. Except no-one wanted the winning ticket.

But the worst was delivering the news to the family of a fellow copper. I knew some life-long police who'd rather take early retirement than face that situation.

"It's your dad. He's dead." Flat. Laying it out there. Figuring she'd understand. She'd appreciate the honesty.

Figured I owed her enough to dial down the drama.

She was silent. I twisted my neck and looked towards her. Her expression was set neutral and her eyes remained locked on the water.

She said, "Dead?" as though she was saying the word for the first time, realising how it sounded coming from her lips.

I told her what I knew. She didn't interrupt. Didn't ask questions.

She didn't cry.

She wouldn't until I was gone.

I took her to FHQ. While she was in there with fellow detectives, I hung around outside in the drizzle. Called Cameron Connelly at *The Dundee Herald*.

"What's up?"

"Off the record," I said. "You heard anything about a copper getting killed?"

"There's rumblings," he said. "We've got Laura Thomas heading over now to ask questions. What have you got?"

"I'd rather not say. Conjecture. Rumours. Nothing concrete."

"Piss up a drainpipe. You know something, McNee."

"I learn anything more, I'll let you know."

"Good. I'll do the same, you know. It's what friends do." I got the feeling there was something else behind what he was saying. He still felt burned after I failed to keep him in the loop on the Furst case several months earlier. "Tell me, McNee," Cameron said, "they done investigating your girlfriend yet?"

I hung up on him.

TWO

Sixteen months earlier, I had been in FHQ, sitting in a windowless room, watching the cameras in the corners and trying not to look guilty.

It's a hard thing to do, of course, when you know you're being watched.

My father had been Catholic, lapsed by the time I was born. He told me the worst part about being raised in the faith was the idea that God was always watching. He told me how he'd been a nervous child because no matter what he did, God could see it. The idea horrified him. He told me one of his friends at school had suffered from constipation because of the fear. "The day I stopped believing," he told me, "was the day I felt free." He escaped the all-seeing eye.

I guess, sitting in that room, I knew how he'd felt as a child.

There would be someone watching, I knew. They'd be watching me to see if I acted like a guilty man. They'd be watching me and analysing everything I did in that room. And that in turn made me start analysing myself, second-guessing every movement I made, even the involuntary ones that most of the time I wouldn't even think about.

I waited. Watched. Stewed.

When DS Ewan "Sooty" Soutar finally entered the

room, I figured they'd either got bored or they'd seen something they thought to be a crack in my armour. Sooty was a big guy. Shaven head. Goatee beard. Used to work as a bouncer before he joined the force. Looked like a rent-a-thug, but was smarter than most people gave him credit for. Used his appearance to his advantage.

He couldn't play that game with me, of course.

He sat at the other side of the table, folded his arms and stayed silent.

I said, "You going to ask any questions?"

He shrugged.

I said, "DCI Bright's watching us."

He shrugged again.

"He shouldn't be watching. He can't be involved in this case. Conflict of interest."

Sooty shook his head and stood up.

I looked at the cameras.

The lights were off.

Maybe the idea was to intimidate me. There wasn't any kind of beating coming my way. I'd worked with these guys for years, and that wasn't their style.

But Sooty had been put in the room to remind me that they could do what they wanted to me. If the fancy took them.

Because I knew as well as anyone that all the regulations in the world wouldn't stop some coppers doing whatever the hell it took to get the results they wanted. It wasn't about good cops and bad cops. It wasn't about right or wrong. It was about getting the job done. And no well-intentioned bureaucratic procedure was ever going to change that.

Sooty left, and Ernie slipped in the door.

We'd spoken briefly earlier that evening. He'd been the one Susan had confessed to.

Her own father.

Read into that what you will.

Now Ernie was looking as though he'd aged years in

just a few hours. The lines on his face seemed somehow to have ingrained themselves deeper into his skin, and there was a stoop to his posture that I didn't recognise. He was carrying a weight around his neck.

He looked at me, his eyes hard and accusatory.

I said, "They're off?" and jerked my head at the cameras.

"We're alone. Say what you like."

I had a lot to say. Settled on, "You have to believe her. She's your daughter."

"And she's always been sweet on you, McNee, in spite of everything."

I took a deep breath before jabbing back: "Afraid she won't forgive you for your faults?"

He smiled, looked ready to break down with laughter. But he composed himself and pulled up a chair at the other side of the table.

"You want to talk about that?"

"You don't know anything, McNee. You're blinded by your own anger. Always been your problem. You get so wound up, you stop looking at the bigger picture."

"There is no bigger picture," I said.

"Have you told her?"

"She knows."

He shrunk away from that. "She hasn't said anything?"

"What do you expect her to say?"

"I brought her up to be honest. To be straightforward."

"Even with you?"

"Especially with me."

We were both silent for a moment. He was the one who broke it. Repeating himself. "You don't know anything, McNee."

"Then tell me."

He shook his head. "Just leave it alone. Give me some time."

"For what?"

"Just leave it alone, McNee."

"What about your daughter?"

14

He was at the door, and he stopped, his hand stretched out, like someone had just hit the pause button on a remote control.

When he turned back to me, I could see he was fighting to keep calm. There was a slight tremor around his arms, his muscles tensed up. It wasn't a conscious thing. He was trying to force back the reaction. But it was tough.

I wondered if he wanted to take a swing at me.

Maybe it would make him feel better about things.

It had worked for me. The day I lashed out at a superior officer. For a moment – and it had only been a moment – I'd felt as though I'd reached a breakthrough with my own worries, as though that one simple act had somehow set me free.

I waited for Ernie to lash out.

Expected it.

But instead, he turned and left the room.

When Sooty came back in, he acted like nothing had happened.

I noticed that was when the camera turned back on.

#

That had been over a year earlier. Now Ernie was dead and I was driving his daughter to the cop shop where she'd have to deal with the sympathy of those who'd worked beside her and her father. Worse still, she'd have to face colleagues who didn't know or understand the situation surrounding her suspension.

Susan was silent as the car slipped through the city. Looking out of the passenger-side window, no expression on her face.

The radio was dialled low.

Maybe she understood that. Knew that any words would be pointless, now.

As we drove past the Tay Hotel – long ago abandoned, now an empty shell – she looked up at the grand old building and said, "Before they moved to Dundee, my mum

15

and dad stayed there a few times. He said that was when he fell in love with the city."

I concentrated on the road ahead, for lack of anything to say.

She said, "They don't know who killed him, do they?"

I said, "No."

She was silent again for a few seconds. "You find out, Steed, you tell me. Alright?"

"Sure."

Blinked a few times. To clear my vision.

#

I parked at Marketgait, outside FHQ. Walked Susan to the main doors. Outside, the wind blew strong. The skies were grey. The city had undergone a severe winter, was only just beginning to come out the other side. During the last months of the previous year, it had been as though civilisation was coming to an end; snow piled deep on the streets and shops unable to open in the centre.

The worst was behind us, but the temperatures were still low.

A headache burned right behind my temples.

Susan told me I didn't have to come in with her. That she would prefer to do this on her own. I offered to wait, but she shook her head. I watched her walk across to the main building, using the doors that were locked to the public. Still acting as though the place was her own.

Someone was waiting to meet her.

Sooty.

I don't think he looked my way.

When Susan was gone from sight, swallowed up by the forbidding, grey 1960's architecture of FHQ, I looked at my watch. Still morning.

There was no-one there to say, so I told myself: this wasn't my case. I had no reason to get involved. Except the worst kind.

And I had a business to run.

Such as it was.

THREE

Third floor, One Courthouse Square. New building, the sandstone still fresh. On the lower floors, there's a building society. To get to my offices you come through a side door, climb an interminable number of steps and bang hard on the door.

I used to have a guy did the admin, but he suffered a work-related injury. Since then it's been a rolling series of temps who never quite have the staying power. Enough of a turnover I was starting to wonder if it was personal.

The latest was a woman in her fifties by the name of Dot. Her husband was retired. Her son, so she said, was a "perpetual student", the description a mix of love and exasperation. No doubt the same tone she used with him. She struck me as the kind of woman who didn't hide the truth.

Reminded me of my own mother.

As I came through the door, Dot handed me a letter. "You'll like this one."

I did.

The letter was from a local woman whose daughter had run out on her fifteen years earlier. I'd managed to track the girl down to a small English village where she'd changed her name and moved in with a man ten years her senior. The daughter had got herself into some trouble at school which was why she had left in the first place. I sympathised. And, in a way, so did her mother, despite her daughter's disappearance putting such a strain on the woman's marriage that she had eventually split from her husband.

The daughter's own life story was extraordinary, and when she came clean to her husband about who she really was, what had really happened to her, I could have wept with him. As it was I felt like an interloper as I stood in their front room, watching the scene.

You never get used to being around people during moments that many believe should be private. The girl had never contacted her mother because she'd been so ashamed at taking what she called the coward's way out. But, according to the letter from the mother, they had a dialogue now. Things were moving forward. It felt good to know that in this world where everything can seem so bleak, there are the occasional happy endings.

After I was done with the letter, I logged on to my email, checked my calendar.

I was working another missing person. There'd been an upturn in such inquiries following media coverage of the Furst case the year before. I turned away most of them, especially while police investigations were still active, but a DS I knew from the old days had sent this particular client in my direction. So far I had turned up nothing on the husband who had slipped out in the middle of the night, but a history of undisclosed gambling debts to local sharks made the reasons clear to me.

Dot buzzed through from reception. "There's a gentleman here to see you."

"Make an appointment," I said. "But make it clear that business is currently backed up and – "

"I think you'll want to speak to this one," she said. "It's David Burns."

Guess I should have expected the cockroaches to come out of the woodwork sooner or later.

"You've had the place done up?" Burns said as he walked through into my office. His tone was upbeat and cheery, like we were old friends. Like this was a social call.

I tried to mirror the façade. It didn't work. So I said, "You know about Ernie." It wasn't a question.

His mood darkened. I took that as a minor victory. He took a seat. Uninvited. "I know about Ernie," he said. "And I know what you're thinking, but believe me when I say that his death had nothing to do with our... friendship."

I didn't believe him.

Why should I? After all the shite he'd put me through over the last few years, he was lucky I didn't just throw him out on his arse. Through the third storey window.

I said, "You came all the way across town just to tell me that?"

He chuckled. "Not even an offer of a tea?" he said. "After the hospitality I've shown you down the years."

I shrugged. Said, "Fresh out." Knowing he could see the teabags and coffee-jars on top of the filing cabinet.

Letting him know the score.

He smiled. Self-satisfied. The urge to smack him one came on strong.

But I resisted.

Call that progress. Maybe I was evolving. Learning how to be a better man.

I didn't know exactly how old Burns was, but he was well past sixty, maybe into his seventies by now. His bullish build was gone, but there was still a power to his body that came naturally. You could see it in the way he moved. A predator, always on the prowl for other human being's weaknesses. He hadn't let himself go to seed. A lifetime of being ready for a brawl had paid off in terms of his health. Two years earlier, he'd been the victim of a particularly nasty assault. You wouldn't know it to look at him. The way he sat, the way he smirked, you'd think the bastard was bulletproof.

In his mind, I think he was.

But all it would take was one good shot to prove him wrong.

He said, "Cards on the table, then. You've turned me down before, but believe me when I say I'd rather have you on the case than the coppers."

The third time he'd offered me employment. Did he expect me to jump enthusiastically at the opportunity? Start wagging my tail like a good little puppy? Fucksakes, I'd turned him down twice before. Sure, some people think a private investigator will take on any old work if there's a cheque at the other end, but most of us have morals.

More than you might imagine.

"It would go against the professional ethics of the Association of British Investigators," I told him. "I'm sorry."

It was a good excuse.

I could point to the relevant paragraph of the charter with my eyes closed.

"Aye, forgive me if I don't follow, son."

Maybe I'd have to get out the pointer. "I mean taking money from a known criminal."

He was silent. As though digesting what I'd just said. Burns was one of those hard-men who had become particularly sensitive about his reputation. He'd lamped a reporter on his doorstep, busting the hack's nose, for merely daring to ask about his connections to a known London gangster.

Mind you, even I had to applaud that particular move. The hack in question had worked for one of the more loathsome rags. It was a wonder he'd even made the pretence at checking up on his "facts".

"Never convicted, lad," he said. "Not proven."

Not.

Proven.

The two most irritating words in the Scots legal system.

During my years on the Force, I'd come to hate the returned verdict.

It's an aberration.

Or, as DI Lindsay might say, a pain in the fucking arse.

Most sensible legal systems have a two tier verdict system:

Black and white.

Guilty and Not Guilty.

Fair enough. Justice cannot have room for grey areas. It must be harsh and absolute if it is to work. Which is why *Not Proven* seems such a waste of time. What it says is, "We know you did it, you prick, but there's just not enough evidence to convict."

It's a verdict that more often than not lets the guilty walk free.

In my opinion, of course.

And the opinion of many coppers and court solicitors.

"That's a slur on my name, Mr McNee. I won't have rumours like that out in the open."

I nodded. Not apologising.

"So I'm here," said Burns, "to ask you to accept my cash. Because I know you, son, you'll be all over Ernie's murder like dog-shit on a shoe. And you can't keep going around doing these things for free. Altruism is an over-rated quality in this world."

"As I'm sure my secretary informed you," I said, "I currently have a backlog of cases and can't afford to take on any new clients at the moment without impinging on those currently engaging my services."

He took the hint, polite and formal as it was. Stood up. Said, "If you change your mind, feel free to call me. Any time. I think you know the number."

When he left, I waited until I was sure he was gone from the reception area. Then I grabbed a mug from next to the kettle and threw it at the wall.

#

He had me.

The old tosspot, for all that I tried to deny it, had a way of getting right in my head. Knew how to push my buttons. And as much as I was aware of it, I still fell for the trick every time.

He'd talked about being the client for a gig I'd just as easily do for free.

He had my number down cold. I wouldn't sit by and wait for the coppers to get results. I'd be forced to look into this by my own nature. Pragmatism would suggest that if someone was willing to pay me for what I would do regardless, then I should take the bloody money. Even if it did come from the proceeds of criminal activity.

Ernie had been my mentor and, no matter what had happened between us, that counted for something. His murder felt like a personal attack.

Not just against me.

But against Susan.

#

Three months earlier, in the days waiting to hear the initial assessment from the Investigative Committee who were looking into Susan's actions during the Mary Furst case, specifically her connection to the death of the psychopathic arsehole called Wickes.

Susan sat with her legs curled up beneath her on the sofa that faced towards the bay windows. She was blowing onto the surface of her coffee, a gesture that was as much habit as it was necessity. The coffee had already cooled.

She was dressed down in blue jeans and a white T-shirt. Every day, I thought her gaze looked more distant. We hadn't talked about her lying to her superiors in order to protect a young girl who made a bad choice.

And, even more damningly, her lying to protect me.

What was there that we could say?

It was what had finally pulled us together.

And threatened to tear us further apart.

"Sometimes," she said, "I think about telling them what I know... what you told me... about my dad."

I thought about her father in the interrogation room, telling me that I need to look at the bigger picture, that I didn't understand what was really going on. I remembered the pained look on his face, the way his eyes had become glassy with tears he hoped to hide, when I confirmed that Susan knew what I'd seen.

He'd looked as though he'd been betrayed.

And yet he was the one who had betrayed her.

When it comes to family, things are never simple.

"But when it comes down to it," Susan continued, "And I'm sitting in that room looking across at the arseholes in the suits, all of them searching for any excuse to find me guilty of some bloody infraction, I think, sod it. His own dirt'll come out one day." She blew on the coffee again. Never once looked at me, even though I was sitting in a chair directly across from her, the heat of the mid-morning sun warming the back of my neck as it came through the window. "And he's my dad. That's the worst part. He's my dad and I looked up to him, respected him. Thought he was a decent man. He was the reason I became a bloody copper, you know that, right? Because it seemed noble. It seemed right. It seemed good."

She had told me before that she couldn't believe what I told her, that there must have been some deeper reason for her father's close relationship with Burns. And once that might have been true, in the days when the Force tried to work with organised crime gangs rather than against them. When they still retained the feeble and naïve hope that they might be doing something proactive and preventative instead of making costly deals with the devil that would never pay out.

Ernie had been part of those deals, once.

Now his friendship with Burns – and I had been there, witnessed for what it was – was crossing a line unacceptable on any level for a professional copper, especially with a reputation like DCI Ernie Bright.

"There has to be something," she said. "Something we don't know. An angle. A play. Anything."

But back then I believed that she was fishing in empty waters.

And I didn't have the heart to tell her.

FOUR

It was late afternoon when Susan called, asked me to meet her at a coffee shop on the Perth Road. One of those places that did fair-trade coffee and home-baking.

When I arrived she was sat at the window, looking out. She tried for a smile when she saw me walk in. Failed. I guess you could say, miserably.

I sat beside her. She inched a black coffee over to me. I took it, letting my hand brush against hers as I did so. A small gesture. Nowhere near enough. Like anything I could do would have been.

I said, "Tell me."

And she did.

#

The story that Lindsay told her was much the same as the one he'd given me.

However, Susan was sure that the DI left out certain details, And it wasn't to spare her feelings; that wasn't Lindsay's style. No, when it came to other folk's feelings he was subtle as a shotgun blast to the groin. And, I sometimes thought, proud of it, too.

"He asked a lot of questions," Susan said. "Like how much I saw my father outside of work, how close we were, whether he'd been acting different lately, all that shite."

I wondered what her reaction had been. She'd talked about his secrets catching up with him, and I knew that Ernie's colleagues – Lindsay in particular – weren't dumb. They had to have known something was up with their boss.

Or maybe they'd put any recent behaviour down to the fact of his wife leaving; an event that had been a blow for Susan as much as her father. Even when you're an adult, there's still a small part of the child inside you that wonders if, in some tacit way, you are to blame for the erosion. If only you had behaved differently they would still be together.

I wondered how Susan really felt about Lindsay's questions. Whether she'd seen them as purely professional, or if she had sensed some personal jab behind them. As though her superior officer was trying to find some way to blame her for what had happened to Ernie.

But Susan was smart enough to know when she was being played. She'd worked alongside Lindsay for a year, had known him longer than that, knew his style when it came to an investigation. He was always one for looking at relatives first, of methodically following procedure and protocol.

Even when his gut might be telling him something else.

I looked at Susan's face. Her eyes were puffed, bloodshot. Her forehead was creased. Feeling the strain.

I wanted to hold her. Just hold her and tell her that everything would be alright.

But instead, I pulled back and said, "What did you tell Lindsay?"

She reacted to that by straightening her back. Looking at me with a strange expression. One I couldn't read.

"I told him what I could. Which wasn't much. That we haven't been talking as much since the Furst incident. That he didn't know what to make of what happened between you and me."

Aye, there was another subject I'd been avoiding of late. We'd fallen into the rhythm of a relationship without thinking about it, without knowing the boundaries or the strengths of what was between us.

But together, I sometimes felt that we were further apart than we had ever been before.

The strain of a secret.

The tension of a lie.

Susan said, "He asked about you, as well. About you and Dad. How you felt about being the Golden Boy and then just another *piece of shite investigator getting up everybody's arsehole*, to quote the man himself." She smiled, the way everyone did when talking about Lindsay's own peculiar turns of phrase, but it was weary and more out of habit than anything else.

The words started to bounce around my head. I should have known Lindsay would try and make this personal.

Ever since I broke his nose – right before I quit the force – he'd gone out of his way to prove that I was a fuck-up, a gobshite, whatever.

Some days, I believed he was right.

Susan sipped at her tea. She said, "I need to go home, Steed. Need to sleep."

I said, "I'll see you later."

She kissed me on the lips. Fleeting, so fast I almost couldn't feel it. Then she got up. Paused, as though thinking about something. "Do I have to say it?"

"What?"

"Leave this to the people who know what they're doing?"

I shot her my best smile, reached and touched her hand.

It seemed to be answer enough for her.

#

The work of an investigator is rarely black and white. Unlike the coppers, you don't have the same moral and legal high ground to dig into people's lives. The various

Freedom of Information Acts that arrived with the dawn of the digital age have served to make our jobs more difficult, despite the clear advantages the digital age has brought to the profession.

Which means that sometimes you have to make friends off the grid.

Like Bobby Soren.

The Grinch, as he liked to be known.

He was the one who hacked Tayside Police's website and replaced the homepage with an animation of a pig humping a rat. As he said later, it was computer code and not artistic subtlety that was his strong point.

The Grinch considered himself a political radical. "I don't harm anyone," he told me once. "I'm like the Banksy of the online world, ken?"

His grandparents had been German, but The Grinch was Dundee through and through. Born in the city, grew up here. He'd run with the last of the Dundee gangs during his youth, and had some scars to show for it. He'd only received, though. The Grinch, as he would tell anyone who'd listen, was "a lover not a fighter". Aye, and he said that in his best Michael Jackson impression, too.

So, The Grinch acted like a dumb prick, but he was always on the ball. The fact that he knew he was smarter than anyone he knew was probably what led to his little stunts. Boredom and frustration can do more to form habitual criminals than any other factor you care to mention.

He met me at a café in the east end of the city. The kind of place where people didn't pay attention to you and where no-one wanted to be noticed.

I grabbed a weak coffee and managed to resist the bacon rolls sitting under the warmer. The fat oozed off the meat, white and thick.

It was hard not to stare.

The Grinch himself was wearing a DUFC baseball cap and a dark tracksuit that hung loosely from his skeletal frame. He grinned as I came over. Half his teeth looked black and rotten. He spent so much time behind a computer screen these days, he'd forgotten how to spell personal hygiene.

"Awright, buddy?"

"You said you owed me a favour."

"More than one."

I sipped at the coffee. Tried not to make a face. "How do you feel about data protection?"

"Depends whose data needs protecting."

I told him what I wanted. He snorted. "Piece of piss. Could do that in my sleep."

I didn't care if he was wired or snoring, just as long as he got me results.

"Aren't there, ken, official channels for that kind of shite?"

I said, "You know I never ask you questions?"

He tapped his nose. Winked. "Gotcha," he said. Like we were partners. Old friends. Comrades in arms.

#

The drug squad have a motto:

Follow the money.

As in, you don't go for the street level dealers, you follow the money as far up the chain as you can and then that's the guy you take down.

I figured if Ernie was fiddling his morals, he would be fiddling his cash, too.

Follow the money.

The Grinch had asked if there weren't official channels I could go through to get my hands on Ernie's statements. And maybe there were, but I didn't have time to waste and more importantly I didn't want to leave a public trail. Not just because I knew Lindsay would be doing exactly the same thing I was. And I knew he wouldn't be too happy to have me pissing on his shoes. Again.

The statements the Grinch pulled – he sent an intermediary to the office with hard copies – went back years.

I spent the afternoon locked in the office, looking at numbers, figures, account details, names. Trying to find patterns, repetitions.

After a while, my vision was beginning to blur. My brain was pushing out against my skull, begging for release from this task. I thought maybe a walk would do me good, but I couldn't leave the room.

I had to keep trying.

Because something in those numbers was going to make sense.

At five, Dot chapped on the office door, told me she was heading home. Asked if there was anything else I needed. I mumbled thanks, told her I'd lock up, let her go.

Too wrapped up in my own head for civility.

Even if I knew I'd end up paying for that later on.

It was past six, and I had sheets full of names and patterns. I'd tried drawing connections, spider-diagrams, notes of all kinds, anything to make sense of what I had.

One name had leaped out.

Mulvaney Wholesale had been paying a regular sum into Ernie's accounts for the last year. They were a front, of course. Mulvaney Wholesale had gone under years ago. Old competitors of David Burns, they'd been subject to what many would euphemistically term a "hostile takeover".

Before Mulvaney, a whole raft of payments came on a regular basis from names I recognised and others I didn't. All companies with dodgy pedigree, but I'd bet you couldn't trace that pedigree in a straight line back to the one man I knew was behind them all.

He was too careful for that. There would be buffers in place. Enough to protect him. The words, *not proven* were a mantra to Burns and his kind.

I didn't bother tracing the payments all the way, although I was sure The Grinch would have given me enough that if

I wanted to, I could. Most of those payments could have been refunds or payouts for moonlighting gigs, and none of them tied back explicitly to Burns. Nothing screamed complicity on the part of a dead DI. Unless that's what you were looking for. And even then, they only whispered surreptitiously.

With malicious intent.

I had to wonder, when did it start?

When did Ernie Bright turn from a man whose moral and ethical compasses were sharply set to a crooked cop who took money from known criminals and drank at their houses as though they were old friends?

#

"We learned the hard way, son, that you can't deal with men like these."

We were in the Phoenix, a pub on Dundee's Nethergate that's become a Dundee institution. The landlord himself was on the bar, had made his usual cracks, asking whether we expected protection money as we walked in the door.

Drinks ordered, we'd grabbed a booth near back of the bar; a small amount of privacy in a public place. The bar was dark, decorated with an appealing eccentricity. The early evening drinks crowd were buzzing pleasantly, even though the pub wasn't quite at full capacity.

The night, of course, was young.

Ernie had been the one dying for a pint at the end of the shift. I wasn't going to complain if a DCI wanted to reach into his pocket, and besides, the Phoenix had been, for many years, my spiritual home.

The day had been a bad one. A probable witness to organised criminal activities had been found face down in the river. An apparent suicide; statements taken at the scene confirmed he'd taken a header off the Road Bridge.

But Ernie knew better.

"It's the way the bastard works," he told me, the bastard being David Burns. "Deniability in everything. Not just to avoid getting caught, you understand, but so he can salve his conscience."

Ernie knew this better than anyone. In the late eighties through the mid-nineties, he had been part of a particularly sensitive police operation that worked directly with some of the most powerful men in the Scottish underworld. The project had been doomed to failure, finally hushed up by the men at the top. Dismissed as a bad idea, or a "fucking failure", as Ernie once put it after a few pints.

Perhaps it was telling that no-one paid an especially high public price for the fuck-ups that were made during those years.

Ernie had told me about this early on during our relationship. "A copper does what is deemed best for public safety at any time. Sometimes you just have to go out on a limb and trust that the man at the top knows what he's doing."

Naïve?

Maybe. But at the same time Ernie was cynical enough to know that the copper who spoke out against the system was the copper who got roasted.

"Times have changed," he said. "We're getting better. Accountability is the new watchword. But that doesn't mean there'll be another sea-change, that someone won't sit up and think the public good might be better served through more... grey-area tactics."

That night in the Phoenix, he was diving right into his pint. The floater's death had got to him. Not because he particularly cared for the witness. But because he knew that he was fighting a losing battle.

Or that's what I believed at the time.

"What this country needs," he said, "is someone to go up against bastards like Burns. Someone with the balls to say, *no more*. Look at us; we're hog-tied, you and me."

I figured he was talking about the fact we had to play by certain rules. Follow evidence chains and ensure our cases followed the guidelines laid down by often archaic and complex Scots law.

But in the months before Ernie's death, I'd think differently about what he was trying to say.

Wonder if we were hog-tied in different ways.

If, in his own way, he was trying to tell me something.

If maybe the pint had been less about winding down and more about trying to get up the courage to admit to some kind of truth.

Or maybe all of that's just wishful thinking on my part.

And I'll never know.

Never have the chance to ask him.

#

There were other inconsistencies, too.

Outgoings that made no immediate sense.

Take out all the expected.

The credit cards, mortgage payments, the monthly bills...

Check the one consistency that remained.

The pattern became clear. Irregular but apparent when you knew what you were looking for. Just like the payments from Mulvaney Enterprises.

The payout always came three or four days after a large deposit. The money moving on fast. To a personal account.

Raymond Grant.

I figured the name for another front, wondering if Burns was somehow using Ernie as another layer to move illegal cash through the system.

Christ, but I felt sick just thinking about what I was looking at.

Not knowing where the money came from.

Or where it was going.

Raymond Grant.

The name was familiar. Somewhere in the back of my head, I could feel the itch. Like I'd heard of Grant before, maybe in passing.

But I was grasping for any excuse I could find.

The desperation of denial.

I stood up, walked away from the printouts and the glow of my desktop's screen. I opened the window to let the night air into the office. It had turned dark a few hours earlier, and in the distance I could hear the sounds of the city; the rumble of traffic, the distant sounds of car horns, the echoes of footsteps on the pavements below. Further down the street, I could hear the chatter of smokers gathered on the streets outside pubs.

I closed my eyes.

Lost myself in those sounds.

Anything so I could forget – just for a moment – the implications of what I had uncovered.

#

When I arrived at the flat, I noticed the Yale was snibbed, but the main lock was open. Slipping inside, I found Susan asleep on the sofa. I grabbed a spare blanket from one of the cupboards, draped it over her.

When she woke up, I was sitting across the other side of the room.

She sat up, let the blanket fall away and blinked.

"What time is it?"

"Past one."

She yawned, lay back down again. "Why are you just sitting there in the dark?"

I didn't give her a reply.

She didn't press.

Within a few minutes, the sound of her breathing changed and I knew that she was asleep.

I continued to watch her for a while.

Was surprised when I felt tears drying on my cheeks.

FIVE

Katie Bright answered the door in a white robe, still rubbing sleep from her eyes. She blinked a few times when she saw me, before suddenly realising who I was and why I was there.

She reached out and wrapped her arms around me. She sobbed, then, and placed her head on my chest. We stood there like that for a long time before she finally pulled back and stood straight, a stance that might have been described as haughty.

She said, "My daughter's not with you?"

I shook my head.

She said, "So come in, Ja –" before correcting herself, "McNee."

#

Katie was a few years younger than her husband, but her age was showing around her eyes. Maybe it was the stress of the last year or so. I hadn't seen her since a few months before she and Ernie split. Even then it had only been in passing. She'd always been kind to me, I remembered, when I used to come round to Ernie's for drinks and a few pointers in the fine art of applying for transfer to CID.

Katie had a pot of coffee already on. She poured me a

cup and we sat in the front room. The flat was on the third floor of a well-maintained block off the Hawkhill, running parallel to the Perth Road. The area spoke of lower middle class money and better-off students.

The windows in the living room were large, let the sunlight stream through. We sat in silence for a while, her on the sofa, me in a comfortable armchair. An observer might have thought us mother and son.

Finally, I said, "When did you find out?"

She said, "Sooty came round. He's a DS now."

I nodded.

She said, "You could have been inspector."

"Maybe."

"He had high hopes for you."

"Why did you leave him?"

With absolute determination, she put her tea down on the glass-topped coffee table. Then she sat back and looked at me with eyes that had won a hundred domestic disputes. "You should be with her right now."

"She's tough," I said. "She's coping."

Katie shook her head and made a clicking sound with her tongue. "You were always good at dealing with people," she said. "Ernie says... he said that about you. But he meant it in a professional sense. Like, you could observe how people were with each other, but... But he also said that you could never relate to anyone on a personal level. As though you couldn't see what was right in front of you." She had a strange expression on her face, her lips moving as though towards a smile they could never quite reach.

I let her talk.

Not wanting to listen. Knowing she had to say something. Like her daughter – and her husband – she was tough. But even if she and Ernie had separated, I knew that part of her still had to love him. And that she would be grieving as much as anyone.

But there was part of me didn't want to hear what she had to say, an impatience tugging at the front of my brain.

An itch. An irritation. I said, "You're avoiding the question."

"You already know."

"David Burns."

"I thought for a long time Ernie had a wee bit on the side. Maybe a little WPC on her way up, something like that. I think I could have coped with that. Maybe. I mean, it's what happens, and it can happen to any marriage. It's not exactly an experience unique to being a copper's wife." She licked her lips. Adjusted her position. Not just uncomfortable in a physical sense. "But when I realised where he was going, the people he was…" She stopped, took a deep breath.

"He didn't tell you?"

She shook her head. "He was obsessed, you know that? Always has… had been. The first murder he ever worked was tied to Burns and the old bastard just skipped off scot free. I guess Ernie always harboured the hope he'd be the one to bring the big man down."

"And then he was sent in to work directly with him?"

"I knew about that. Eight years. He hated it. Or that's what he used to tell me. And he hated himself, too for doing it. For not speaking up. For accepting it as his duty." She spat out the last word as though the very taste of it disgusted her. "When he came home at night, he would always take a long shower. Standing under the water for hours at a time. The ceiling paint used to crack with all the steam. I knew what he was doing. Washing any trace of that man away."

What she told me tied in with what I'd always believed about Ernie Bright. That he was at heart a principled copper, that he'd done some questionable things in the name of the job, but that he had his own personal lines and that he hated himself for ever having had to cross the line.

"You don't think he…?"

"No," she said. She stood up. "And you can go to hell for

even asking." She composed herself, taking a deep breath. Said, "Do you care for my daughter?" as though we hadn't talked about anything else.

I hesitated. Waiting for a trick, sensing that somehow she wanted to trip me up here.

"Yes."

"Then what are you doing here?"

Trip.

Crash.

Right over on my arse.

#

Everything in life comes down to the choices you make.

Sometimes what you do will have an immediate effect. At other times, you wind up waiting for years see what the consequences will be.

But it's true. Once you've made a choice, you're lost if you don't stick with it.

Maybe it's something in my upbringing. Something in my childhood that made me stubborn and determined, a dog who won't let go of the stick he's just run after no matter what.

But something in Katie Bright's question shook me. Made me wonder whether I was displacing myself with this investigation, whether I was trying to avoid the reality of the situation.

Susan's father was dead.

What could I do about that?

What was I trying to achieve by investigating his death?

I sat in my car for a long time thinking about this. People walking past looked at me, maybe wondering what I was doing sitting in this street, not moving, staring straight ahead, my hands not even on the wheel, my lips not even moving as though talking on some hands-free device.

Finally, I moved. Reaching out to my phone and dialling in a number.

Straight to answering machine.

"This is Susan Bright. I can't answer right now. Leave a message."

I left a message.

"Call me when you get a chance."

I think my voice cracked on the last word.

#

Back at the office I started work on a speech I was preparing for an ABI conference later in the year. Anything to distract myself. I was talking about *Technology and the Modern Eye*, discussing how an investigator needed to adapt and change to a modern world where information was allegedly available to even the most casual of civilian inquiries.

Not that I believed that to be true. In most cases, straightforward use of Google is destined to fail even the most basic of inquiries. Yes, we have the technology to do most of the work that people would have relied upon private contractors to do in decades past, but computers, for all their magic, still require a degree of skill for them to be effective. And that is where investigators can still hold the edge.

I had my central arguments planned, topics laid out and research sitting in folders. But I couldn't concentrate on the task at hand. Found myself flicking between open windows on the computer, reading and re-reading the same material.

Finding none of it connected in my brain.

Like I was merely scrolling through word-soup.

At half-ten, Susan came up to the office, dressed in jeans and a baggy jumper of mine that she'd recently adopted. It looked good on her. Better than it ever had on me, anyway.

She said, "You called?"

I made her a coffee.

We didn't say much.

39

She sat in my leather-backed swivel chair and nursed her mug. Finally: "It sounded important. The reason you called."

"It was," I said. "I'm sorry."

"For what?"

"Making this about me. For turning your father's death into..." I let the sentence hang there.

She nodded. "He meant a lot to you. In spite of everything. And... you know that you meant a lot to him. At least, you did..."

I said, "He was your father."

Susan sipped at her coffee. Tentative. She let a little pass her lips, winced, and blew on the milky surface of the liquid.

I said, "What I'm saying is, if you need anything, I'm here."

"We've been here before. Where you say you're going to stay out of something that doesn't concern you and then you dive right back in."

"People change."

"Not compulsives." She said it with a smile. Like a joke. Delivered in earnest. "What I'm saying Steed, is that if I need you, I'll yell. From the rooftops." She put the barely touched mug back down on the desk. "But I know you. You need to feel like you're doing something. And if you need to poke around and get that out of your system I'm fine with that." She walked over to me, and kissed me quickly on the lips. It was a brief and fleeting touch, the kind of sensation where, when you think back on it, you're not sure if you really experienced it.

When she left, I stood there for a long time, thinking about what she had said.

Then I went back to the computer, closed down the files I had open. Dug into a password-protected folder.

ErnieBright.odf

I double-clicked. Looked over what I had.

Thinking, this was what I had to offer.

This was who I was.

SIX

Susan was back at the flat. When I walked in, she was lying on the sofa, reading a paperback. I checked the cover. *Choke Hold*. Looked lurid.

She noticed me, smiled, marked her place and put the book down. Said, "That kid in Waterstones who does the crime books recommended it."

"Any good?"

She grinned. But it was false. I wondered if she'd even noticed what she was reading. These days, it seemed everything Susan did was displacement activity.

I understood.

Empathised.

Didn't know what the hell to do.

Susan left the room. I heard taps running, the kettle boiling.

I waited for her to come back.

When she returned, I noticed how tired she was looking. Pale and unwell. Her eyes were puffy and her skin was near-porcelain in colour. I walked over, put my arms around her.

She squeezed back, but it was perfunctory and she stepped away after a few moments.

I thought about the last few months.

How we were closer. And yet further apart; our relationship like an Escher painting.

Susan sat on the sofa. I remained standing.

She said, "They want me in again, tomorrow. Professional standards."

"Did they say if they were any closer to a decision?"

She shook her head. "Ask me, Dad's death only makes it look worse."

"It's a separate incident."

"Come on, Steed!" she said. "You're not naïve. You know how this works as well as anyone."

People used to ask me about when I left the force, *Did you jump? Or were you pushed?*

"What are you going to do?"

"What can I do? Go and talk to them."

I sat down on the armchair opposite Susan. Looked at her.

She told me she'd made an appointment to see someone, a counsellor. But she hadn't gone. Another talk we'd never had. There were a lot of them. Things that needed to be said. The problem was, neither of us had the nerve to bring the subject up first.

I said, "Does the name Raymond Grant mean anything to you?"

She creased her brow. I couldn't work out if she was thinking about the answer to the question or trying to work out why I'd even asked it in the first place. "What's he got to do with anything?"

"Then you know him?" Without thinking, I'd gone into interrogation mode, no longer talking to her as a friend or a lover but more like a source.

"Yes," she said. Was there a catch in her voice? An irritation? "He... he worked with Dad when he first transferred to CID in the eighties."

That was when it clicked.

"Why do you want to know?"

I shook my head. No sense saying anything yet. Until I knew more. Until I understood more.

Susan got to her feet. She came over, stood above me, then leaned down and kissed me gently.

Held the gesture.

Reached down and took my hands. Guided them.

I wanted to say something.

Knew what she was doing was displacement.

But I let her take control.

It was all I knew how to do.

#

Later, Susan slept beside me.

It was past three in the afternoon.

I heard a buzzing from the floor. Rolled over and reached down to my jeans to pull out the mobile.

A text.

Unexpected.

I slipped out without waking Susan.

Knowing that I couldn't explain where I was going.

Not today.

#

Rachel was sitting at one of the window seats in Drouthy's, soda water and lime on the table in front of her. I ordered myself a Coke from the bar, sat across from her.

We didn't say anything for a few moments.

I could see in her face that this was more than a social call. Every time we met like this, I felt a shiver run down my spine. She reminded me so much of her sister. Yes, there were differences, but the set of her mouth and the tilt of her jaw always made me think of Elaine.

For a long time that was why I avoided her. Believing that by not thinking about Elaine and how she had died, I could make the pain go away. Believing that Rachel served as a reminder of things I would prefer to forget. It was stupid, foolish and selfish. But it's easy to say such things with the detachment of hindsight.

I would come to realise that sometimes the best way to

deal with something is to face it head on. Of course, knowing that and doing something about it are two very different things.

We hadn't seen each other in maybe seven months, Rachel and I.

Nothing personal. Mostly down to business. On her end as much as mine.

I opened the conversation. "You're not usually so terse."

She didn't smile.

"Dad's ill. Cancer."

Tried to find the right words. They didn't come.

"He's known for some time. Hid it from the rest of us. Made Mum swear not to tell."

"I'm sorry."

She sipped at her drink. "He didn't want you to know."

"Why not?"

"You and he are... on better terms... but, you have to understand..."

"I do."

On better terms.

Talking her way around the fact her dad had tried to have me arrested following Elaine's death. Like I killed her deliberately. Orchestrated the crash as petty revenge for an argument we were having.

The driver of the other car had never been caught. Meaning the only person Martin Barrow had left to blame was me. It was only a few years ago we had reached anything close to reconciliation. I think he only forgave me because Rachel wanted it. Because I was the only link any of them had left to Elaine.

I didn't talk about her. About us. And I'd been avoiding any of her family since Susan and I finally...

Rachel said, "I thought you needed to know. A while back I said that you were family. I meant it."

I sipped at my drink. Watched past Rachel, outside, the people walking by. Students hanging on the steps of Duncan of Jordanstone Art College across the road. The sky was grey, but the air was warm.

I said, "How's the Weegie?"

She grinned. I was talking about her husband. Reformed Glasgow hard man. So he said. I didn't see any of the tough guy to him, if I was honest. Maybe he felt the patter was his to uphold; a kind of civic pride in the tough, Glaswegian image.

Then again, one of the things being both a copper and an investigator had taught me was that you should never judge by appearances.

"Last time he was in the city, mind," she said, "two bastards lamped him one. He's taken against the place."

"So he's never coming back?"

She didn't say anything.

The silence hung between us.

What did we have in common without her sister?

Even when Elaine had been alive, I had never felt truly at home with the Barrows, even though they did their best to welcome me. But I think we both knew that I'd rather have been anywhere but at family gatherings. I wasn't a family man. Would never be.

Rachel said, "I shouldn't have called."

"No," I said. "Please... I just... there's some shite happening and..."

She smiled. "Same old McNee," she said. "Burying your-self in your work. In other people's problems. Avoiding the responsibility of having a life of your own."

I held up my hands in mock surrender.

She kept smiling.

SEVEN

Raymond Grant.

It had been years since anyone on the force last talked to him.

Decades since he and Ernie had been friends.

Grant, after all, was a corrupt cop. Who the hell wants to associate with a corrupt cop? Or, at least, one who's been outed.

I remember Ernie mentioned his name once or twice. The same way you might talk about a cancer, with that barely restrained hate tripping off the word.

I would have figured that to be the reason he and Ernie quit their friendship. Except for the fact that the morning after Ernie's death, the papers were trumpeting:

DEAD POLICE DETECTIVE: CORRUPTION ANGLE?

Fast work, especially for the local hacks. I figured at least one of them had a source on the inside. Whatever, the new Chief Inspector would be throwing a fit over that one. Part of her pledge when she took on the job was an assurance that all coppers on the Tayside payroll were above reproach.

No matter how you spun the situation, it was going to look bad. For the force. For her pledge.

It was early morning when I drove across town, heading

for the estate where Raymond Grant had lived for the last six years. I was turning off Lochee Road when the mobile rang. I took the call through the hands-free.

"What the fuck are you doing?"

Lindsay.

"Working."

"Aye, at what?"

"I don't have to give you my itinerary."

"Correct me if I'm being a cunt," he said, "but you look like you're heading for Raymond Grant's place."

I checked the rear-view.

Recognised the monkey behind the wheel of the unmarked that was running up my arse.

Could have run myself off the road right then.

#

We stopped off at a nondescript café. Other than some scattered OAPs who probably lived at their tables, we were the only people in so early.

The old woman behind the till didn't look too happy to have customers actually sitting in. Probably figuring it meant dirty dishes and more work for her.

She also didn't appreciate at least one of us being a copper.

Lindsay would never have made a candidate for undercover. Had the police vibe all too easy, rolling off him in waves. You'd need to be blind not to see him for what he was.

He ordered at the counter, got a scowl for his trouble. Came back with two coffees and two limp-looking bacon rolls.

"They'll set you up for the day," he said. "Or else they'll kill you."

"Nothing like gambling your life on breakfast," I said.

"The joy of traditional Scottish cuisine," he said, dousing his bacon with tomato sauce from an unmarked red squeezy-bottle. I figured he'd be lucky to taste the meat beneath that. Then again, maybe that was the idea.

I watched my own roll. Wary of signs of life. And grabbed the bottle from Lindsay when he was done.

Lindsay said, "You want to tell me what you want with the corrupt old bawbag?"

"Susan remembers Raymond. He used to be close with Ernie. And then one day he just stopped coming round."

Lindsay nodded. "Probably when he got found out."

"She reckons before that," I said.

Lindsay sipped at his coffee. Made a face. "Put fuckin' hairs on your chest," he said, then looked over my shoulder at the woman behind the counter and gave his best smile. The one that made him look like a shark at feeding time. He turned his attention back to me. "You didn't blink when I said you were going to Grant's."

"I have my sources."

"This was being kept internal."

"Why are you on this and not D&C?"

That got him. He hesitated. Told me a lot. Lindsay never hesitated. Never doubted himself. "D&C are looking for a corrupt cop. You and I both know..." he hesitated again, and I realised it wasn't because he was doubting himself but because he was confiding in me. It was choking him to admit anything to me. "Fucksakes, we both bloody well know Ernie was a lot of things. But he wasn't corrupt."

It felt good to hear someone say it. But, did we really know that? I thought about seeing him at Burns's house. About the doubts I'd harboured over the last year. I said, "You think you know someone. But..."

"Don't you dare! Don't you fucking well dare, you wee shite," he said, leaning over the table, jabbing one of those overly-long fingers in my direction.Keeping his tone low, close to a whisper.

I said, "I want to believe he's innocent. I do. But –"

"– But what?"

I hesitated. If I told him what I knew, I was shitting on

Ernie's memory. But if Lindsay was going to conduct anything close to an effective investigation, he needed to know everything.

He'd have said the same thing, too, if the tables were turned.

"But we have to be open to the possibility that he was involved in something."

Lindsay shook his head and sat back again. He said, "Tell me why you're not with your wee girlfriend right now?"

"I can't leave this one alone."

"Why not?"

"You once told me that Ernie was disappointed in me. Fine. I accepted that a long time ago. But I didn't stop thinking of him as my friend or my mentor." I had to tell Lindsay what I knew. Sooner or later it was going to come out. He had to know everything "But some things have made me start to doubt what I thought I knew."

"Such as?"

I took a breath. "Last year," I said. "I saw him at Burns's house. Not there on business. A guest of the family. He was there, drinking wine in the back yard."

Lindsay took it better than expected. Maybe he'd just been waiting for me to actually say it. Already knew what I had to tell him, just didn't want that confirmation. "This is what you didn't want to say?"

I licked my lips. My mouth was dry. I wasn't so sure I wanted to drink the coffee, though. I said, my voice cracking, "He was in with Burns, and I didn't want to believe it. I figured he was playing an angle."

"But?"

"He wasn't. None that I can see."

Lindsay said, "And none that I've heard about." His voice was soft, his tone clipped. Restraining himself. Back when I was on the force, we all knew that it was when Lindsay stopped the bluster and went quiet that you really had to worry.

"There has to be something," I said.

"You want him exonerated?"

"Aye."

"For your peace of mind?"

"And Susan's."

"Right," said Lindsay. "Don't forget the daughter." He looked about to say something else, but caught himself at the last moment.

I said, "Okay, so my interest is personal." No shame in admitting it. No need to cover it up.

"Personal's bad," said Lindsay. "Personal fucks things up."

Telling me something I'd already learned the hard way.

#

Raymond Grant's one-bedroom flat was the bottom floor in a decrepit 1960's estate. Walkways connected the upper levels. The décor of choice was spray paint and slaggings:

Josh eats cock.

Kelly is a lesbo munter.

Street poetry, you might call it.

Avant-fucking-*garde.*

There was no-one around. A few curtains and blinds twitched.

People inside probably saw Lindsay, saw *copper*, and decided it was best to stay inside. Maybe when they saw me, they saw the same thing. It's something that never really leaves you. An attitude. A style. Something that screams to the world who you are or what you've been.

Grant's front door had been hit by the spray-can artists.

Peedofile

Twat

Smelly auld cunt

Slogans overlapping, intertwining.

Minimalist. Hardly Banksy-level. But effective in getting their message across.

Lindsay knocked hard. The copper's knock. The kind of knock that touches something primitive in the back of your brain, makes you feel guilty even if you've done nothing.

I hung back. Acting like I was grateful to be along for the ride. Guess I was, in my way.

"In the end," he'd told me, before we left the café, "I'd rather have you where I can see you."

Whenever Lindsay turned his back, I fought the urge to fire off the finger. Old habits die hard.

We waited for an answer.

Lindsay knocked again.

Finally, the door opened a few inches. Cautious. A face peered round the crack. Maybe only a quarter visible, but enough to see the tired, leathery skin, the watery, bloodshot eyes and the greying stubble of a face that hadn't seen a good razor in a long time.

Lindsay said, "Raymond Grant?"

"The fuck wants to know?"

Lindsay held up his ID.

Raymond Grant said, "Jesus Shite," and opened the door all the way.

EIGHT

Grant led us into his living room. We would have sat down but for the washing that lay scattered across the sofas and chairs. Grant shoved some onto the floor so he could flop into a tired, beige armchair. His heating was up full blast, four bars of the gas firing red.

I looked at Lindsay.

He was sweating hard. Didn't make a move to loosen his tie.

Grant said, "What do yous want?"

Lindsay said, "Time was, you were a copper."

"Aye," said Grant. "You could say that."

"Hard fall."

"You come round here to gloat?"

"Why would I do that?"

Grant belched, loudly. Didn't even have the decency to look proud. Just sank deeper into the chair. There were old stains on his trousers. When did he last put on new clothes? Just how long had all this laundry been lying around the flat?

There was a smell of damp. Mildew.

And another faint scent underneath that stung the back of my nose and crept down my throat with malicious intent.

Lindsay said, "Do you read the papers?"

"Fuck would I want to do that for?"

"Friend of yours died yesterday."

For the first time, Grant looked away from Lindsay and at me. "Who's he? Where's his ID?"

"My friend here is consulting on the case, privately."

"Get to fuck."

Lindsay moved fast. Down, grabbing at Grant's collar, pulling the old man up and out of his chair as though he weighed nothing. Given his near skeletal frame, maybe that was true. Lindsay got his face right in the other man's, kept his voice low, controlled, righteous. "Listen to me, you sack of shite, I don't have to be fucking nice to you about this, because this friend of yours who died, he was a copper. You get that?" He pushed Grant away again. The old man stumbled, crashed back into the chair.

I hung back near the door. Trying to appear disinterested. Wondering if maybe Lindsay had brought me along for appearance as much as to keep an eye on me.

Who said the coppers don't use the same tricks as the criminals?

I wondered if Burns's goons felt any conflict about the things they saw. If they had any kind of conscience.

Grant sputtered a few times after landing back in the chair, finally, said, "Jesus fuck, man, okay, okay! You're talking about Ernie. Aye, I fuckin' remember him, so why're you here?"

I figured I was done playing the strong, silent type. Stepped forward. "Checked your bank account recently?"

He flinched. As though from a slap.

Lindsay wasn't prepared to give up the lead: "We know about the cash. So tell me, why was he paying you money, you wee prick?"

Grant shook his head. "No," he said. "No, no."

I slipped into the background again. Grant kept looking past Lindsay to me, unable to work out who I was and what I was doing here. Maybe the years off the force had begun to have an effect; my attitude no longer saying "copper" in the way I believed it did.

"Hoy," Lindsay said, "Bugger-lugs!" Got Grant's attention. "Don't look at him. He's no interest to you. I'm the only bastard you want to be focussed on, aye?"

Grant said, "Need a smoke."

"I give you one, you going to talk?"

Grant nodded.

Lindsay turned to me. "Well," he said. "Give the man a bloody ciggie."

I took a pack out of my inside pocket. I'd quit a few years back, but one of the tricks of the trade is to always have something you can barter with. Two things you can always use to get people talking: cigarettes and alcohol. Like the old *Primal Scream* song.

I tossed one to Grant. He caught it with the accuracy of desperation. He fumbled in his pockets for a lighter.

If you're a smoker, the truth is that the craving never really goes away. Most ex-smokers I know have either got uptight about the whole affair or replaced it with something else. I found that occasionally reminding myself of the reasons I should quit tended to work. And men like Grant were living examples: the shakes, the sunken eyes, the rotted, yellow teeth.

Not all attributable to the cancer sticks, of course.

But it felt good to tell myself that they were.

As he sparked up, Grant's sleeves shifted a little and I caught a glimpse of his stick-like arms, the exposed tracks both old and new. His flesh a veritable pin-cushion. Raymond Grant didn't strike me as the type to go in for acupuncture.

Grant moved to the window. Old wooden frame, single glazing. Looked as if a good breeze would blow them in.

He said, "It should have been him."

"What should have been who?"

"Bright. It should have been that bastard got his arse handed to him. But he was too good."

Lindsay said, "Listen to me, you little toerag, I've had

enough crap today. And you're talking about a friend of mine. A colleague."

"Aye, whatever," said Grant. He blew smoke out in an unsteady plume. "Hit me if you like. Doesn't change anything."

Lindsay said, "Why was he paying money into your account?"

Grant hesitated. "We were old friends," he said. "I mean, he was helping me, aye? Get back on my feet."

"Balls," Lindsay said.

Grant looked at me.

Lindsay said, "Keep your eyes on me, big man!"

Grant dropped his cigarette on the bare floorboards. "What do you want?" he said. "Does it bloody matter what I tell you?"

"I want the truth."

Grant was shaking. It could have been the drugs. How long since his last fix? He was jonesing, maybe.

It was a sad thing to see. From what I knew, Grant had once been considered a good policeman, a rising star. He and Ernie had worked well together, and on the rare occasions Ernie had mentioned Grant, his voice had been tinged with a kind of sadness; a regret at a life wasted. Where had he fallen? Had it been one long fall or hundreds of tiny stumbles that led him to this shitty little flat, bumming cigarettes off men who hated him, trying to pretend no-one could see the pockmarks on his skin or the glaze on his eyeballs.

Grant leaned against the windowsill to stop his trembling. He said, "I don't have to say anything to you. I don't have to tell you anything." He held out his hands, wrists up. "You want to arrest me, aye fine, go ahead. But I've said all I'll say to yous. Do you have a fucking charge?"

It would have been easy to put the aggression he'd displayed throughout our little chat down to drug use. But there was something else, I was sure. A deeper motivation, something we just couldn't see yet. He didn't want to answer our questions.

Because he was afraid.

Not of us.

But of something else. Or *someone* else.

#

Outside, I said, "He knew we were coming."

"Bloody right he did, the arsehole. But he had a point. We can't just arrest the bastard on a gut feeling. What he said earlier, that Ernie was giving him money out of some kind of bastarding good-Samaritan guilt complex, it's something we can't disprove. Not right now. But I feel it in my gut, that there's something he's holding out on us.

Feel it in my gut.

Gut feelings had seen friends hurt and nearly got me killed.

Gut feelings had made me shoot one man in cold blood and wind up covering up the murder of another.

And here I was, again, like Lindsay, trusting that twisting sensation in my stomach that told me, *something's wrong.*

I said, "You saw his reaction when we pressed about the money. He panicked. Might have been the drugs, but I don't think he was high. Not today."

"I'll not deny that one."

Jesus, Lindsay was going to make me work for it like a newly minted detective on fucking probation. And he was going to enjoy it, too.

"He knew we were coming."

"Maybe the washed-up prick just doesn't like dealing with coppers," said Lindsay. "Understandable given what he –"

"No," I said, as we reached the car. "That wasn't what it was about. He didn't want to talk about Ernie. He didn't want to talk about his past. He didn't want to talk about the money. Somebody got to him. Somebody told him to keep schtum. He'd rather we arrested him than he talked."

"Aye, you've got a point," said Lindsay, walking to the driver's side. "Somebody gave him a real bastarding shite of a fright. There was blood on his shirt, too." He grinned at me. "Use your eyes, McNee, you might make a detective one day."

He unlocked the car. Stopped just before opening the door, looking as thought he'd just seen something at his feet. "Oh, get to piss!"

"Something wrong?"

"Some wee bawbag's taken my fucking hubcaps."

I did my best not to look too happy.

NINE

I climbed in my own car, parked just behind Lindsay, hit the radio.

Whisky in the Jar-O

Made me think about Martin Barrow, Elaine's father. He'd been a Thin Lizzy guy, I remembered.

Christ, I was thinking about him in the past tense. As though he was already dead and gone.

I'd got the feeling, when talking to Rachel, that she was having the same thoughts, feeling as guilty about them as anyone. But it was only natural that she was preparing herself for the worst. At least she had the time to prepare, to accept what was happening.

Time was, I might have envied Martin in a strange way. For a long time after Elaine's death, I had become wrapped up in my own feelings, completely selfish and absorbed with my pain. Unable to rationalise it, I had started looking for ways out, ways to end everything. The word *suicide* never crossed my mind. But the way I acted, that's what I was considering, what I was looking for.

I had Martin's number in my phone.

While we'd never be best friends, we had started talking again. Forcing ourselves past old grudges and anger.

All I needed to do was press a few buttons. Say a couple of words.

I'm no believer in the afterlife, but if Elaine had been watching, she would have appreciated that. She used to tell me, "You don't have to like people, but you could at least try." Saying it like a half-joke, but always serious beneath the smile.

I could have dialled the numbers. Could even have made the promise that I would do so later. But instead I switched stations and put Martin Barrow out of my mind.

Telling myself I had more pressing matters to consider.

Like Ernie Bright.

And Raymond Grant.

Someone had got to him. Lindsay and I had seen the same things. Whoever it was, they'd got Grant to clam up on what he knew about why cash had been flowing from Ernie's account into his.

The way he acted, we figured he was more scared of them than of us. And why wouldn't he be?

We were coppers, after all. Or at least one of us was. There were rules we had to follow, boundaries we couldn't cross. All the bluster and bluff in the world couldn't change that.

I had to wonder why someone would lead us to Grant and then scare him into not talking about what was plainly obvious; a trail of breadcrumbs left out in the open air. Of course his denial looked like he was hiding something, maybe even trying to protect Ernie.

Was I reaching out in desperation? Seeing conspiracies because I wanted, more than anything, for Ernie to have been the man I once believed him to be. All the evidence pointed to a dark truth, to a copper who had gone over the edge, but I had to cling on to the belief that someone wanted Ernie's death to look that way, to distract from the truth.

Paranoia?

Was I looking for vindication?

Or merely praying?

Rain spattered down. Dundee weather: temperamental at

best. Sometimes I thought the city could shift the atmosphere on its own; as though they were indicative of a shifting mood. Which made Dundee as close as you could get to being a depressive; periods of unrivalled sunshine followed by unexpected and sudden bouts of downpour and dull.

The rhythm soothed me.

I had my hand on the keys, but I wasn't turning.

Who had got to Grant before us?

What were they hiding?

Was I so wrong about Ernie?

I closed my eyes, let my head fall back against the rest.

Who had got to Grant before us?

If they had got to Grant, then who else – ?

Sodit. We'd just walked away, like good coppers, because we knew we were beaten, that our rules prevented us from doing what had to be done.

But I'd seen the way that Grant looked at me. Edgy and uncertain. Not sure who I was.

Certain I wasn't a copper like Lindsay.

Wondering if I had to play by the same rules.

I dialled in a number on the phone.

"What?"

"Give me ten minutes," I said. "Then I want you back at Grant's place."

"Christ, McNee, leave this shite to the professionals."

"You want him to talk as much as I do," I said. "You're the one who said you'd rather have me working with you. And you know I can do things you can't, walk places you're shut out from."

"You can't touch him," Lindsay said. "You even give the bastard a scratch, I'll have you down for assault before you take another breath."

I said, "Just trust me."

Lindsay didn't say anything. Just killed the call. I took that to be a "yes".

#

60

Briefing room.

Early morning.

Years ago.

Seeing the memory from a distance. As though it belongs to someone else.

Maybe twenty of us, wired on early morning caffeine and lack of sleep. A few hangovers. Easy to tell who was a candidate for hard-core alcoholism.

I was in the third row, still a plod, maybe six months away from transfer and hopefully promotion. CID was the goal. The dream. The ideal. The reason I'd joined up in the first place. It was ten months before Elaine's death. A year and one month before I'd break DI Lindsay's nose and finally quit the force.

Looking back, I realise how unlikely it seemed, how no-one could predict any of what happened.

The world only ever makes sense in hindsight.

In my memories, I am young. Little more than a kid, really. If you ask me what ī look like, I'd say I look the same as I did at nineteen. I think I'm grown up. Back then, I knew nothing about the world. I just thought I did.

Ernie Bright was up front. Standing before a projection screen.

Talking Serious and Organised.

Talking witnesses.

Talking David Burns.

"The problem is not that we don't know what he's doing, it's that we can't link him to any of the shite that happens in his name."

Beside me, a guy who wears glasses and looks out of place in uniform makes copious notes. I don't know his name, but figure he's shooting for promotion and desk.

There are two types of coppers, or so I believed.

Those who want to get their hands dirty.

And those who want to let others do the hard graft.

Glasses was one of the latter.

And that was fine. Every organisation needs someone

standing back from the field, directing the plays. As long as they can appreciate the realities of what that means for the front line grafters.

"The few witnesses we've ever had have failed to provide conviction. For a variety of reasons." Ernie clicked through to an image of an older man wearing Mr Magoo frames. He was frail, as though he'd get blown away by an early morning breeze. "This man came forward with a promise to link Burns to drug trades out in the Lochee area, and a whole network linking back to Eastern Europe. At the last moment, he had a change of heart, said he'd made a mistake. He was willing to serve time for perjury. Nothing we did could make him change his mind." Ernie stopped there. He looked at each one of us, as though we could answer the question he was about to ask. "What happened?" Another pause. We all knew the answer, but we let Ernie say it out loud. "He was more scared of what Burns and his boys would do than he was of jail time. Because he knew that we operate within certain guidelines. We can only intimidate up to a point. And while we hear stories about coppers crossing the line every time we open a newspaper, the truth is that most criminals – and most members of the public – know such instances are rare." Another click. Another image. A woman, mid-forties with fair hair and the kind of eyes you'd call piercing. Like a bayonet. She had a proud bearing, held her head high and stared right at the camera as though daring it to make something of her.

"Kate Fairweather. She came forward after one of her sons was killed. The lad worked for Burns – off the books, away from his legitimate public work – and wound up dead for his trouble. Part of a little gang trouble we had in the late nineties, a skirmish that cemented Burns's dominance in the city. The lad was killed, execution style, a clear message. His mother took it hard, decided that enough was enough. The worst problem with men like Burns – the manipulators, the liars, the users – is that ordinary people don't see the pain these men cause until it's too late. Ms Fairweather couldn't save her son, but she was determined she could save someone else's. Or at the very least take revenge by helping put the man she held responsible behind bars."

Glasses scribbled furiously.

Anecdotal detail adds flavour to procedural notes, but you rarely need it. Even then I knew the lad didn't have the chops for street work. His attitude screamed, *Facilitator*. Of course, he'd probably go far. Further than me, at any rate.

"There are some witnesses who cannot be intimidated. Ms Fairweather was one of them. She kept in close contact with the investigating officers. Told us of several attempts that were made to buy her silence. And then she disappeared." Ernie was trying to keep his tone authoritative, but if you knew the man, you could hear the stresses and cracks in his voice. He'd been one of the investigating officers. A lifetime spent trying to put men like Burns away, and this had brought him so close.

Was that what sent him over the edge?

Was there something in my memories of him that I had overlooked? Were there signs that he was not the man I thought he was?

It's easy to rewrite memories.

Refocus them.

Remember what you want. Add retrospective details. Make sense of your past, even if it is a kind of lie.

Another click. Crime scene photographs. Stark. Sharp. Brutal.

Check the reactions around.

From stoic to steeled to stunned.

A couple even leaning forward, like they needed to see.

Go into this line of work, there are always ghouls.

I looked at Glasses. He'd quit scribbling, couldn't look away.

Ernie clicked through:

Another angle.

Click

Another.

Even the ghouls shifted uncomfortably. All of this become real to them. More than just the kind of horrific pictures young men laugh at to prove their masculinity.

"No-one was ever arrested. Lines of enquiry were followed, but petered out. Men like David Burns pride themselves on working without a trace. They also pride themselves on their ability to bully and intimidate. People are scared of them because they work outside of the law, outside of the rules that ground the police and the authorities. The biggest threat men like David Burns face is from witnesses, from those who trust in the system. Testimony is key if we are to take men like this down. We cannot allow –" *click* "these –" *click* "atrocities –" *click* "to continue."

Click.

Click.

Click.

#

In my head, I clicked through images. Same way Ernie had done with the overheads so many years ago to reinforce the power and emotional effect of what none of us had been there to witness.

My mind filled in the details. Created images I had not seen.

Click

Overhead, Ernie on the floor of the warehouse, his body twisted.

Click

His eyes. Glassed over.

Click

Blood pooling on the concrete floor.

Click.

Click.

Click.

I knocked hard on the door.

"Open up, you bastard!"

Hammering.

To wake the dead.

When the door cracked an inch, I followed through with a shoulder shove, the door swinging hard on its hinges and knocking Raymond Grant off his feet. I stormed inside, pulled him up on to his feet and threw him into the living room.

He stumbled, crashed over the tiny coffee table hidden under a pile of sheets. Maybe they cushioned his fall.

Pity.

"What the fuck, man?" His voice was broken, pathetic.

He trembled when he spoke.

I noticed the works near the window.

Fresh used. Our visit had rattled him enough he probably didn't even wait until we'd closed the door behind us to dig out the stash.

I walked past him, picked up what was left. "Naughty boy, Raymond."

"Personal use." His voice was shaking, the tremor of fear clear and unmistakable.

I picked up Grant's works, threw them at him.

He cowered.

"You can't do this. There are rules." But he didn't sound sure. I was an unknown quantity to Raymond Grant. That gave me the advantage.

One I intended to exploit.

"Aye," I said. "Last time I was here with a copper. Now, it's just you and me, you prick."

He was crouched on the floor. Like a parody of the Igor character in the old black and white Frankenstein movies; a pathetic, half-formed man cowering in terror and fear.

Did I feel sorry for him?

Knowing the things he had done?

I looked at him cowering.

Thought about Ernie Bright bleeding out, alone, in a warehouse.

His life and reputation destroyed.

And this man knew why.

This man who had screwed his life every step of the way. Who had thrown himself into the deep end of life and never tried to swim back to the surface.

I said, "There were others here before us."

He nodded.

"They scared you. Threatened your life."

He nodded again.

I said, "They didn't lose a friend the other day."

Let him think on that.

He was crying, now. Trying to hold it in. Shivering all over. Hard to tell if it was guilt, fear, or the need for another fix.

Maybe all three. Like I gave a toss. All I wanted from him was answers.

Telling myself I wanted them for Susan.

That I was doing this because it was the only thing I could do to help her, now.

Aye, check the hero complex. Threatening a pathetic old prick who's been paying for stupid mistakes his whole life, who must have thought every day about welcoming death. Why else would he be sticking shite in his veins if not to welcome the embrace of the eternal high? Close to death as you can get without actually toppling over the side.

Some people numb the pain with chemicals.

Others with anger.

He stuck a needle in his veins.

I lashed out.

Make your choice.

Looking at him, I suddenly felt a wave of nausea. Not at him, but at myself. For thinking I could come in here and beat the truth out of someone like this.

No better than the people who'd told him not to talk to the coppers.

Grant looked up at me. Trembling.

I said, "Fuck it," and stepped past him, out into the hall.

Opened the front door, found I was blinded by the light outside.

Heard a voice say, "Wait. You fucking prick, hold it. I'll tell you about Ernie. About the other bastards. Whatever. The fuck does it matter, anyway? I'm going to die one of these days. Maybe they'd be doing me a bastarding favour."

I stopped.

Turned back from the light outside.

To talk to the dying man who lived in the dark.

TEN

Raymond Grant just wanted to be left alone.

After his dismissal from the force, he existed on anger. At himself. At the force, who tossed him aside like an unwanted tissue. At the world which he felt owed him *something* for the sacrifices he had made.

But he had no focus.

No drive.

"Where did I go from there? Christ, how do you pull your life back together after they tell you you're a disgrace to society? How do you pull yourself up and become a human again when no-one's willing to give you a bloody chance?"

He found he had no contacts in the straight world who would speak to him. At least when I left, I did so in a tide of anger, but not of shame. Grant had nothing from his old life that he could turn to.

And his reputation – a crooked copper – followed him into the jails and beyond.

He served his sentence, isolated from other prisoners after an incident that resulted in damaged kidneys and hours of emergency surgery just to keep him breathing.

In prison he learned despair and hopelessness.

Applied those lessons to the world outside.

Applied them well.

Lived his life in the flat. The walls were the boundaries

to his world. He never wanted to venture outside.

"Used to keep the place clean, you know? Like I still had a life?"

But he didn't have one. He couldn't have one.

While he was inside, his wife filed for divorce. The one person he thought would never abandon him, "But I was being a fucking eejit. I would have dragged her down with me." And his daughter, too. "She'll be twenty-six years old, now. Last time I saw her, she was this tiny wee thing. Big eyes. Big brown eyes that looked up at you and said, 'Protect me from all the bad people in this world.'"

I let him talk at his own pace.

No more threats.

No more fear.

Sometimes in this job, you're less an investigator and more of a psychiatrist. Or a priest. Go about your job the right way, people want to talk to you. Like somehow you'll be able to forgive them for the things they've done.

For some things, however, I've come to realise, there can be no forgiveness. Not from an outside party. The only person who can forgive you, the only person you should confess to is yourself.

All the bad people in this world.

Grant was one of those bad people. Or he had become one.

Maybe he even realised that back then.

His public fall from grace, when you looked at the facts, was instigated through a series of mistakes that became more and more blatant.

Like he wanted to be caught.

Like he wanted to be stopped.

Guilt is a strange thing. An emotion we don't always recognise straight away.

He told me about his fall from grace.

I listened.

How his life crumbled.

I listened.

He told me how he was not alone, but he was one of the officers targeted because his behaviour was noticed. "Policing changed. Aye, maybe for the better. And you either went with it or you got your bollocks ripped off by the new Disciplines and Complaints bastards."

Did he think he could continue to get away with his behaviour?

"I don't know, son. I don't fucking know. Ken, now we'd say it was a mental problem, that I just couldn't stop the same old fucking behaviour. But I dunno. I dunno."

Like I said, some folks thought he wanted to be caught.

Guilt.

Fucks us all up in ways we don't expect.

I asked him who else was involved. Anyone who was never caught.

"Y'mean Ernie?"

"Tell me about him."

Grant, his body hunched, his voice stammering, his mind finding it hard to focus for so long, shook his head. "You don't want to know. I saw what happened earlier when – "

"Tell me."

"He moved with the times."

"And before the times moved?"

"There was a period where we wound up on the same squad, attached to Serious and Organised."

"Targeting David Burns."

"Know how we used to deal with the big boys? We let them break the law within limits. Because here's the truth that this brave, new, politically correct world can't handle: we're better off knowing who the criminals are and what they're doing than letting them slip underground and off the radar. Human nature is fucked, son. Bad people will do bad things. We can't stop it."

I said, "But you can control it."

"Aye," he said. "That's what we tried to do. On fucking orders, too."

I thought about what Ernie had told me about the bad old days when the brass tried to strike deals with men like Burns. How the line had started to blur between copper and criminal, and when the whole operation fell apart, how everything turned to chaos.

I remembered him telling me how hard it had been to approach Burns as an equal, how it had been equally hard to overturn a carefully nurtured relationship.

Aye, maybe too hard?

Grant wasn't telling me anything about Ernie.

Like he was afraid it would somehow hurt me.

As he talked, he periodically pawed at his face with the backs of his hands. His eyes were roadmap-red, and he was having difficulty breathing. Sounding like an asthmatic. In the stifling atmosphere of his flat, I had to wonder about his health, how he kept on going like he did.

I said, "Tell me about the money. Tell me about why Ernie was diverting money from his accounts to you."

He lowered his head. Body trembling. I expected him to start rocking back and forward. Maybe throw in some drool for effect.

But the trembling was as far as he got before, "Isn't this cosy?"

Lindsay.

Later than expected. I'd been thinking maybe he'd decided to walk away. Either thinking I was full of bluster or thinking I wouldn't get anywhere coming back to see Grant.

But I didn't register my surprise. I didn't move except to turn my head, see him in the door.

He stood casual. Screaming *smug* in his posture and expression. Those lips twisted. He couldn't smile properly, not something that came naturally to him, but he did a fair enough smirk when he wanted to.

I said, "Just having a wee chat."

"Right," said Lindsay. He came in, stood beside me. Calm and smiling, his gaze focussed on Grant. "Thing is about my eejit of a friend here," talking about me, "he forgets the arrangement we made this morning. You know we just want to get to the bottom of what happened to your old partner, aye?"

Grant was still, now. Transfixed by the DI. A mongoose confronted with a snake.

Lindsay had something under his arm. He threw it on the coffee table.

An envelope.

"Raymond," he said, "I want you to look at these. Tell me if you recognise anyone."

He'd clearly had his own ideas after our chat with Raymond earlier. I wondered where he'd been, what was in the envelope.

Grant didn't move. Refused to look at what was in front of him.

"Raymond," Lindsay said, in soothingly soft tones, as though talking to a nervous child, "If you don't look at these photographs in the next thirty seconds, I'll rip your fucking arms off and beat you to death with them."

Raymond got the hint.

Emptied out the glossies. Looked at them carefully.

Laid out three so that we could see them.

"They were the ones came to see me."

Lindsay gathered up the images. "I were you, Raymond, I'd maybe think about moving."

He touched my shoulder.

I took the hint. Had seen the photographs and realised their significance. Realised Grant had given us all he could.

The poor, washed-up old bastard.

ELEVEN

Down the road, we walked into a public park. Sat on a bench that was shaded by a pathetic old tree whose branches were bare, skeletal.

The wind came in from the Tay.

Cold.

Made me shiver.

I spoke first. "They're coppers."

Lindsay said, "You recognise any of them?"

"Seen at least one of them around FHQ," I said. "Not enough to speak to. They're all young. Joined after I left, maybe."

"This whole case is a fucking disaster. I had a feeling about it since this morning. When there's one rotten apple, it usually spreads through the barrel."

"We don't know –"

"We know that someone's rotten, McNee. I know you think me and Ernie didn't get on well, that I'd be fucking happy to see the pain-in-the-arse get posthumously sent down for shite he might have tried to hide in real life. But the fact is I really don't want him to be dirty." He took a deep breath. "Let's face it, though: some fucker's bent. Someone set him up at the very least, and to do that they need connections on the force."

I was feeling tired. Limbs heavy. Just wanted to go home, hide under the sheets and forget everything.

But it was too late. I couldn't back out. For my own sanity as much as anything.

"I'm not a paranoid prick like you," Lindsay said. "I don't see conspiracies around every corner. But this morning, we both knew that Grant was scared of someone, that we weren't the first bastards to approach him about Ernie. Maybe he's been scared for a long time. Whatever story he had ready for us about how Ernie gave him that money, I think it was bollocks. I think someone's been setting this up for a long time and they knew we'd follow the trail, make the connection between Ernie the veteran bastard detective found with all that cocaine and his doped-up junkie tosspot ex-colleague."

I was thinking, *Burns*.

Lindsay told me what he'd figured, "You were going back to talk to him. Fine, gave me a chance to do some thinking. One of my instructors at the college works for Discipline and Complaints. Owes me a favour or two."

"That's where you got the pictures?"

"I won't tell you what the bloody price was."

"I won't ask."

"Thing is, McNee, this is going to get big. If Ernie was mixed up with those bastards, this is serious shite. There's a major investigation in the works. One of the reasons the old man gave me access to those files. If we can bring one of these boys in, maybe D&C can squeeze them. Make a deal." He made a face, then, and spat on the ground. "The squirmy cunts they are."

#

Grant had picked out three faces from the array.

Constables. None of them veterans. Which was why they stood out. I'd been expecting long-serving officers, but what I got were fresh faces.

They were nothing more than foot-soldiers. Errand boys.

But they were a start.

The first looked like he could barely shave; a round-faced lad named Cal Anderson. Anderson had already been marked as a potential trouble-maker. Despite that smooth skin and baby-round face, he had been cited several times for excessive force and for the sloppy, inconsistent quality of his arrest sheets.

The second was the spit of the Pillsbury Dough-Boy. Robin Reed didn't have as thick as a jacket as Anderson, but he was being looked at for social connections. He'd grown up in one of the city's more colourful areas, and most of his schoolyard contemporaries had gone on to work for the likes of David Burns. Reed had kept his nose clean, but there were questions being raised concerning his arrest rate and the number of convictions that had fallen through in his name.

Contestant number three was the senior of the group. At forty-one, Daniel Hayes was married, with two children. A career copper. With a career that had gone nowhere.

Read:

Malcontent.

Cynic.

Whatever.

Somewhere along the line, his record had gone sour. But it was his bank account and lifestyle that became of interest to Discipline and Complaints. Hayes was living the life of a man whose career was going places, not stagnating among the rank and file.

All three men were under covert investigation. Along with twelve other officers Lindsay's contact had given him.

But these were the three that Raymond Grant picked out.

Our first lead. The loose threads we could tug on.

We.

Lindsay was troubled by that word, too. I could see it in his face. He'd barely tolerated working with me when I was on the force. Now that I was an outsider, the idea went against every instinct he had.

And yet here we were.

Like he said, he'd rather have me where he could keep an eye on me. And in a way I thought he might be right in that regard.

#

"You're not worried about your reputation?"

"Like any prick in the station house liked me to begin with?"

"Some people respect you."

Lindsay nodded, but I'm not sure he really agreed. It was just a way to get me to shut up. "And what I'm doing is –"

"Investigating your own."

"Christsakes, what, you think the thin blue line really matters? That all boys in blue stick together no matter what? Discipline and Complaints are a necessary evil. Most bastards just like to moan about them because they're a pain in the arse. Not because they break the bloody brotherhood."

Did he sound convinced of his own argument?

I couldn't be sure.

Hard to think of Lindsay as a human being sometimes. I had my set ideas about him. Who he was. What he represented.

I always approached my work thinking that the truth was never what my clients expected, that there was always more to people than what one person could see.

Never really applied that yardstick to myself.

I saw Lindsay as an obstacle. An enemy. A one-note, sweary bastard. A throwback to the Neanderthal copper from the bad old days.

I knew he was a father. Didn't matter to me, didn't register, because somehow the kid didn't feel real. As though in my heart I believed Lindsay had invented a family just to fit in with the rest of the human race. Yet I was watching him as he talked about investigating fellow coppers, and despite his constant mantra, that it was *all part of the job*, I could sense the conflict that manifested in the involuntary muscle twitches around his eyes and the way his breath caught momentarily at odd moments.

And what I had begun to realise was this:

He'd gone out of his way to help me. Where I might have thought all he would want to do was hinder.

I said, "So tell me what we do."

"You," he said, "you bloody well go home to that girl-friend of yours. Be a man about it, too, show her you're not a complete prick."

I could hear something of the father in his voice, suddenly, the way he might speak to his young son. Beneath the bluster, all he wanted was for people to see the world as he did, because if we did, maybe we'd do the right thing.

I realised he cared for Susan.

Not in a romantic way. But I knew they'd worked together on more than a few investigations. Susan had always tried to convince me Lindsay wasn't the bad guy I took him for.

Maybe he really had been the good guy all along. Maybe I'd been looking for my heroes in all the wrong places. Or maybe I was just too tired to think straight.

I stood up.

He said, "Grant won't talk to anyone about what you did. He's too much of a cowardy cock."

I didn't say a word.

After all this time, *thank-you* would ring hollow between us.

TWELVE

When I got back to the flat, Susan was looking through old photograph albums. Had them spread out on the living room table. Leaning forward, looking at grainy images from the past.

I sat beside her. She didn't look up.

She pointed to one image. A young-looking Ernie – he'd been a handsome chap back then, with dark, wavy hair and a clean-shaven, angular face that accentuated those sharp eyes his daughter had inherited – with his wife and daughter, sitting on a wall, rolling countryside stretching out behind them. Susan was somewhere around five years old, with an insane bowl haircut and the mischievous look of a child who was going to break all the rules she could get away with.

She said, "That's how I think of him. Even when he got old, when we hadn't seen each other for a while, I'd always be surprised for a moment when he didn't look how I expected."

I reached over and touched her hand.

She used her free hand to turn the page.

More images. Family holidays. Smiles. That grainy quality of the cheap, 1970's camera.

Memories.

Everyone had them.

I kept mine locked away. For reasons of my own.

Susan said, "You ever think about your parents?"

I studied the photographs intensely. "How's your mother doing?"

She smiled, somewhat sadly, as though at a distant disappointment. "Well as can be expected. Surrounded by sisters and nieces."

"You're not with them?"

"I stayed a while. Needed to get away."

"Do you want me to – ?"

She said, "Stay," and turned her hand so she could grip mine. We stayed like that a long time.

She told me about each photograph. Every memory it evoked. She spoke slowly, as much for herself as for me. Sometimes she'd get this smile playing about her lips, but it would fall away fast as though in deference to the present.

Only later would I realise that she didn't cry.

#

The night was drawing in. I had ordered Chinese from the *Mandarin Garden* on South Tay Street. Gave me an excuse to take a drive and collect.

I needed to sort my head. Figure where I was. The last two days beginning to blur.

I left the radio off.

Drove in silence.

Like there was something more I could have done.

But even if I got to the truth, maybe Lindsay had a point when he said what I really needed to do was be there for Susan.

Our relationship was still tentative; each of us dancing around the other, as though worried about certain truths we'd hidden for years.

The first time we'd slept together was shortly after Elaine's death. Something we both regarded as a mistake.

79

The counsellor I'd gone to see after the accident might have said that I was looking for some form of comfort, that our reaction had been almost healthy. Or maybe I was putting words into his mouth as an excuse for my behaviour.

It had been years now, since then. Susan and I had drifted apart, and then come back together; victims of circumstance.

Circumstance.

Coincidence.

It had been events that pulled us together. Terrible events. Grief always seemed to bring us closer.

After Elaine's death, we had slept together. More out of need for comfort than anything; an expression of something we couldn't put into words.

But that had, in the end, only lasted for a moment before we found ourselves pushed further apart than we had ever been. We stopped talking. Started avoiding each other. As though the idea of what we had was something to hide from, to be ashamed of. Until a suicide that forced us to work together.

And then the missing girl.

Mary Furst. Fourteen years old. Taken by her birth mother in a misguided attempt to save her from a psychopath. I'd been looking into the girl's disappearance as a favour for a friend. Susan had been part of the police investigation. Our paths crossed. Both of us witnessed a tragic end to events, as a young girl did something she would regret forever.

A moment of rage.

A bad choice.

One made in a moment of grief and horror.

I had been ready to lie on behalf of the girl. Until Susan beat me to it.

I still didn't know why.

That was the catalyst, bringing us together again in a way that seemed inevitable; a natural act neither of us could deny. There was no point I could say where we entered a relationship. It just happened. Neither of us realising.

A shared trauma?

Or something else?

But sometimes the physical aspect of our relationship felt more like a barrier than anything else. As though somehow it pushed us further apart than we had ever been. And neither of us knew how to get past that. Or else we were scared to.

#

Back at the flat, we ate in silence, the TV providing background noise.

Soaps. Local news. Didn't matter. I don't think either of us were really paying attention, welcoming the excuse to become lost in our own thoughts.

At some point, after we'd cleared away the leftovers, Susan kissed me. When I pulled away, she pushed in. Putting her fingers through my belt loops and pulling me against her. I gave in. We both welcomed the moment. Lost ourselves in it.

Together.

And yet apart.

#

Susan slept on her side, facing the window. She had most of the sheets. Bunched them up around her, gripping tight as though afraid someone would steal them away. I didn't mind, I tended to get too warm at night. I liked the coolness of sleeping above sheets.

Not that I slept easily.

It had to come at some point, but most nights were spent staring at the ceiling, trying to force myself to relax.

I turned my head and looked at the bedside clock.

LED numbers burned.

2:30am

Another light exploded in the dark. A buzzing noise. The thump of a vibrating phone. I reached out, grabbed the offending device.

Not mine.

Susan's.

Display said: *Lindsay (Home)*

I nudged her. "For you."

She reached up, slow and sluggish. Answered the phone with a mumbled hello, not quite able to form the words. But then she was sitting up, feet over the edge of the bed, sheet falling away from her, revealing the curve of her back facing me. Her hair fell loose down the nape of her neck.

"Aye? ... What? Slow down... Jesus, Annie, what do...? Okay, okay... I'll be there."

She hung up. Put the phone down next to her. Put her head in both hands, let out a long, slow, sigh.

I stayed where I was. Wanting to reach out. But doing nothing.

"What's wrong?"

"DI Lindsay... George..." She stood up, moved to where her clothes had been thrown onto a chair by the window. She started to dress, slowly. "He's been attacked. I don't know the details... he's in the hospital. That was his wife. She says... a coma, Steed. She says he's in a bloody coma."

THIRTEEN

DI George Lindsay.

Rumour was they used to call him "Curious" George due to his simian features. Fair enough. It was kinder than what the coppers who came up through my generation called him.

Some days you can't remember why you started a spat with someone. It's just a fact of life. Me and Lindsay had been at each other's throats for years. More or less since I started on the job. Call it a clash of personalities. Some people even implied we were similar.

Both of us called bollocks on that.

I remember when they told me that he was the lead officer in the investigation into what happened to Elaine. That he was the one charged with finding the bastard who'd knocked us off the road. I felt as if I'd been betrayed in some way. And Lindsay did nothing to try and dissuade me of that belief.

I thought that he hated me. A true loathing. And why wouldn't I? A lot of shite had gone down between us. Our professional relationship was best described as blunt. Personally, we were antagonistic, if you wanted to downplay it.

I didn't think Lindsay was the right man for the job. I honestly believed he'd see the assignment as one more chance to fuck me over. It was a melodramatic reaction, perhaps. I can't claim that I was thinking or acting rationally back then.

People talk about how grief can be like a temporary insanity. Which was how I wound up breaking Lindsay's nose. Ostensibly, I had other reasons for striking him, but mostly I did it because I was convinced he'd done nothing but sit on his arse and let the trail go cold, leaving me with no clue as to who had run the car off the road, killed my fiancée and left my life shattered.

I had convinced myself that Lindsay had allowed Elaine's killer to disappear out of spite, some held-over grudge that I couldn't pinpoint but still knew existed between us. Nothing dissuaded me of that idea for a long time.

But in the last few years, as much as I tried not to notice, I'd seen another side to the DI. Perhaps it was Susan's influence. After all, following her transfer to CID, she'd wound up working closely with the man. She tried to repair our relationship, tell me the truth as she saw it; that George Lindsay was a dogged, determined professional who, as it happened, just didn't have time for the niceties of everyday life. According to Susan, Lindsay took his professional life absolutely seriously. Prided himself on results. And even if he had personal feelings, he didn't let them interfere with a case. An assignment. A duty.

Maybe she was right. Didn't mean I liked him any more, though.

In his younger days, Lindsay had been in the army.

I don't know much about it, but it was the talk around the force. Rumours persisted he'd been a candidate for the Special Forces, but had walked away for reasons no-one seemed too sure about. Difficult to tell by looking at him whether these rumours were true. He seemed too small and scrawny to have had SAS potential. But then you saw him work on an interrogation and you realised how he was hiding something underneath that frame. A power and anger you didn't expect.

I'd once described him as simian. Meaning it as an insult. The way he carried himself and that high forehead made him look like the missing link resurrected.

I forgot to remember that a monkey can rip your arm off if the mood takes him.

It was strange to think of him in hospital. Lying there. Still. Silent. Broken. I'd become used to the idea of Lindsay being around. Not that I'd started to consider him a friend. But he'd become a familiar obstacle. An expected opponent.

A sparring partner.

Which might explain why my stomach was churning as Susan and I walked through the main doors at Ninewells.

This time of the morning, the reception area was quiet. Walking past the shuttered clothes stores and the darkened *WHSmith*, I felt as though I was trespassing. Hospitals are odd enough places during the day, but at night there is a strange expectancy in the air, as though everyone has gone home to avoid whatever stalks the corridors in the dark.

The woman on the front desk was pale, a walking cliché of the night shift. Slightly overweight, with the years showing on her face, and grey hair that might have been curly if she let it grow out. She looked at us with undisguised disdain, and asked why we were here.

The only visitors at this time of night came with the worst news.

Who could blame this woman for being a cynic?

Susan asked after George Lindsay, and the woman's face softened suddenly. As though she saw something in Susan that told her we weren't ghouls from the clean-up crew.

It was just as well the woman didn't give me a second glance.

I don't know what she would have seen.

We turned off, grabbed a lift. Inside, the space felt too

large. Designed to move patient beds around with ease. Susan grabbed my hand. And squeezed.

Yet kept her distance.

Let go when the doors slid open.

We walked down the corridor. A nurse stopped us. Susan said, "I work with George Lindsay."

The nurse – mid-thirties, a tough face and tired eyes – said, "You and a hundred other bloody police." She jerked her head down the corridor, "We've got a special room set aside. Incident room." Those last two words just the right side of sarcasm.

Walking down the hall, I heard the voices low and angry.

Didn't recognise anyone right off.

How long since I'd socialised with the boys and girls in blue?

Most of them would cross the street rather than say hello. Some sense of betrayal over my departure. Like I'd broken more than just one man's nose.

In the first few months going private, maybe I'd burned more bridges than I thought. But I'd been full of anger, past caring about such things. Not seeing the road ahead. Maybe this evening would salve some bruises. Heal some rifts.

Or maybe not.

I was barely in the room when a bullish man whose name I couldn't recall looked at me, and said to Susan, "Not your boyfriend."

"I just want to know –"

Sooty was there in the room. Still the same intimidating presence I remembered, his hair shaved down to the bone. He stepped forward, gently nudging the bull to one side, and said, "He's still breathing, McNee. Your wish didn't come true."

Sooty and I used to drink together on Friday nights. We hadn't talked since I left. Except that one time in the inter-rogation room. My fault more than his, of course. I take responsibility for my own behaviour, the way I treated people.

Like I said, I hadn't smelled the burning wood of those bridges at the time. Or hadn't given a shite if I did. And there was nothing I could do to change any of that.

I said, "I'm not here to cause trouble. Lindsay and I had been working on –"

Sooty always had a temper, a violence that raged just beneath his skin. This evening, he couldn't hold it back. He roared as he stepped towards me.

We embraced violently as he rushed me out into the corridor.

I tried to push him away.

My feet went off the ground.

I cracked back against a wall, my spine twisting.

Muscles spasmed.

I beat down on the back of his head. Fists bouncing off the flesh of his neck.

Heavy fists pounded my sides. Aiming for the kidneys. For whatever they could slam.

The world broke into areas of dark and light.

Shapes lost cohesion.

There was a rush of sound, like a violent sea trapped in a shell, echoed in my skull.

I was aware of other people around us. Some of them were yelling. I couldn't make out the words.

The pounding stopped. It was sudden and unexpected.

I tried to remain on my feet. Wound up slipping down the wall, my legs folding, concertina style.

I took deep breaths.

Sooty was crouched next to me. Holding up fingers. "How many?"

I turned my head away.

He said. "Maybe its best if you go outside for a smoke, huh?"

I said, "We should grab a pint sometime. For old time's sakes."

He said nothing. Just stood up.

I saw Susan standing a few feet away. Her eyes met mine and I tried to figure her expression, but she turned away too fast, her arms folded.

Hurt worse than ten-pound punches to the kidneys.

#

The thing with giving up smoking is that sometimes without it, you're left at a dead end.

It's a great time killer.

Cigarettes: the procrastinator's pal.

I read somewhere that when the smoking ban hit, people started striking up relationships because of shared ground outside where cold weather and sharing of lighters led to romance.

Smirting, they tried to call it.

Buzzwords. The bane of the modern world.

But whatever labels you wanted to use, the smoking ban brought people together. Smoking can be good for relationships. More than that, it's a damn a good exit strategy. Need an excuse for a sharp escape? Smoking works. "Just stepping outside." Words more magic than "abracadabra". Didn't really matter how long you were gone, either.

So, aye, there was part of me wished I still sucked on the cancer sticks. Even if I knew the risks.

Because, simply walking out of that ward, with no other excuse, I felt like I was giving up. Admitting defeat. I had no excuse, no reason to present as a mask. I was merely slinking away after having my arse handed to me.

In the elevator, I leaned back against the rear wall and let loose a long sigh. Exhaling hard. My head smacked back against the metal box.

I welcomed the shock.

On the ground floor, as I passed the woman on reception, she looked up with a challenge in her face as though daring me to ask her something.

I didn't.

Just walked down the long entrance hall and out to where the taxi-ranks and buses bustled during the daylight hours. At this time of the morning, however, the space seemed eerily empty. Automated tapes announced the rules of smoking on hospital grounds and asked me to dispose of my ash carefully. If I was in a biblical frame of mind I could have believed the commandment that seemed to come from nowhere was the voice of God.

Even if I smoked, I probably wouldn't have listened.

I walked round the edge of the hospital, following the concrete path laid for pedestrians. At this time of night, as you disappeared out of sight of the main roads, walking maybe ten feet parallel, there was an odd feeling of isolation.

I felt a light sweat prickle down my back, following the path of my spine. My fingers started to spasm. There was an odd sensation at the back of my neck; an itch I could never scratch. Like being stuck in a dream where you were waiting for something bad to happen. That sense of the terrifying and the inevitable.

The night air was cool, a slight breeze sharply brushing against my exposed skin. I put my hands into my coat pocket. Kept walking.

Thinking about what had happened. The attitude I'd faced in the hospital. Could I blame them? One of their own had been brutally beaten, and they didn't have a clue who was to blame.

I could relate.

To the lashing out as much as anything.

Remembering how it felt just to turn and throw out a fist. All my anger and hatred directed in one motion, one moment. Like I was throwing it away. The resistance as I smashed my knuckles into Lindsay's face. The way the bone cracked. The warm gush of blood over my fingers.

For just a moment, I had felt at peace in a way I hadn't done for weeks. And there was quiet. Peace. But it was quickly lost. Becoming something I could never quite regain. Just a vague notion. A sensation that passed me by.

I had, for the longest time, tried to find that calm again again. Thinking if I could find someone to blame for all the evils in the world, if I could have revenge on them – a justified and perfect kind of revenge – then maybe that feeling would stay with me forever.

They talk about five stages of grief:

Denial

Anger

Bargaining

Depression

Acceptance.

I got stuck somewhere around number two. For the longest time. I don't remember stage three. Or four.

Maybe I just went straight to five.

But I'm still not sure I'd say I ever accepted anything. Except maybe the notion that there was nothing I could do to change the world.

Maybe five really led to four. If you thought about it too long. Wallowed in your own world.

Stage two was where I had felt most alive. Anger giving me purpose.

Sounds perverse, perhaps, but in those days I had felt a clear, singular purpose. An absolute sense of right and wrong. Self-destructive in its way, but it had washed away all the doubt and uncertainty, left me feeling focussed and unafraid.

Less given to thought. More to action.

Susan had said I was looking for suicide without admitting it.

Others said similar things. Some had even tried to help me. But the clarity and the drive had been intoxicating. It was an addiction and I wanted another fix even if I knew on some level I could never find something so pure as that initial burst.

As I walked through the hospital grounds, I felt something surge in my veins. A small kick that was intoxicating in its familiarity.

I remembered how my life had been a search for causes, for events and people that would focus my anger. Was I experiencing something similar on Lindsay's behalf? Feeling something like sympathy for a man I had professed to loathe?

"Hey!"

I turned around.

Cold wind pushed against my face. Snow was starting to fall from the skies. Winter drifting in early.

I had just crossed a footbridge that spanned the hospital drive, took me across onto a sloping path that led back to the city. On the other side, from where I had come, a figure stood on his own. He was dressed in a heavy jacket, a thick woollen hat protecting his head against the night air. His breath came out in a long stream. When I was a kid, during the winter months, we used to pretend we were adults smoking in the cool air, miming cigarettes and blowing out steam.

The man was big, even beneath the black Puffa jacket that accentuated his shoulders. He stood with the legs-wide, head-forward stance of a bouncer anticipating aggro.

He said, "You're McNee." A statement or a question? Did the distinction even matter to him.

"And who're you?"

He took a few steps forward. "A man with some friendly advice."

The accent was local. Born and bred in the city. Maybe not the west end, though, where those with money and the middle classes tended to migrate. He sounded more Fintry, or maybe Kirktown. Whatever, a place where people took pride in their roots, and where they stayed through the bad times.

His first few steps had been slow and deliberate. Maybe to deceive me. Maybe to prolong the moment. But then he made the rush. Was on me fast.

Several inches taller, he looked down on me with barely restrained disgust. Like I was a bug, and all he wanted to do was crush me with one heel of those old Docs that looked well-worn and broken in.

Probably on someone's skull.

He said, "Your wee friend didn't take the message."

"Wee friend?"

"Get to fuck, pal. You know who I mean."

"The DI and I aren't exactly friends."

"Aye? So that's why you and him have been poking your noses where they don't fucking belong. Know what happens to noses that get poked in the wrong places? They get broken."

Hardly poetry, but he got the point across. Can't say as though I cared for what he had to say, though.

The snow fell heavier. The snowflakes got caught in the light of street lamps and the bridge lights.

The man's face was shadowed strangely. Like those old movies where they wanted to make the bad guys look mysterious.

Time seemed to slow for a moment. I took in the details, the jagged rock of his nose, the curve of his lip, the old scars not quite faded.

I recognised him.

He was wrapped up, sure, with the jacket zipped right to the top and that hat pulled down over his lumpy skull, but it clicked with me that I'd seen him before.

This man wasn't a simple thug.

He was a bloody copper.

FOURTEEN

Three faces.

That's what Lindsay had shown me.

Three faces. Three files. Three compromised cops.

And now I was face to face with contestant number one. Cal Anderson.

I said, "Not exactly a professional attitude, Officer Anderson."

He growled.

I couldn't be sure whether the noise was instinctual, or if he was going for effect. I figured the former. This man wasn't given to theatrics. One look at him, you knew that he lived for the violence. But he took it straight up. It was about the visceral joy of the moment.

In short, he wasn't the type to indulge in foreplay.

Thugs like Anderson have two choices in channelling their natural instincts. They can become crooks. Or they can become coppers. Sometimes the line between the two personality types is less distinct that the public would like to imagine.

Anderson had wound up playing both sides against the middle. If I had to guess, I'd say more by chance than forethought. I didn't think he'd give me an answer if I asked.

He said, "Aye, good one. You know who I am. Think it's going to make me go away? Tail between my bloody legs?"

"Think no-one's watching you? Think no-one knows what you really are?"

"Fuck you, pal."

"You know the Complaints have a fat file on you?"

"Fuck their file." But he hesitated for a moment, like this was the first time the thought had occurred to him. He was trying to figure out whether or not the idea scared him.

I pressed the idea deeper. "Whatever you're involved in, it's not too late to back out."

Aye, great idea. Like prodding a tiger in the eye with a sharp stick.

Anderson grabbed my jacket collar.

In the movies, I always laugh when someone gets hauled off their feet. It looks stupid. Utterly unreal. Yet Cal Anderson managed to yank me into the air. For a moment. Enough to twist his body and chuck me against the safety barriers.

I could have toppled over. It was a miracle I managed to stay on the right side.

He came towards me. A bull preparing to charge.

No, not a bull. Some kind of cat with its prey. Bastard was toying with me.

"Come on," I said. "You're going to be hauled up for assault and battery of a fellow officer. That's bad enough, but –"

"Fuck it," he said. "Think anyone cares what happens to you?"

He was a big man. But stupid. A good brawler. If he landed a punch, you were going to feel it. Probably not feel much else for a long time.

But he was so big, he telegraphed every move. Couldn't help it. It came to him naturally. This wasn't like fighting Sooty, a man who used his brains as much his brawn when it came to a scrap. No, this eejit might as well have had big neon signs spelling out his next move. And besides, I was expecting this guy to make a move. With Sooty, part of me had been stupidly hoping he would be big enough to forgive and forget.

Just call me a believer in the best of human nature.

As Anderson made his move, I ducked and shifted to the right. Couldn't have gone left if I wanted to. Not enough power in my right leg to do that. The cold was causing my joints to seize up, and old injuries still haunted me no matter how often the doctors tried to convince me they were psychosomatic in nature.

A few months earlier, I'd attended an ABI retreat with an emphasis on personal protection. The convener had been a woman named Zoe. She had taught me several valuable lessons.

One: the toughest person in the room is actually the slight, inoffensive blonde woman who doesn't waste time boasting how tough she is and just shows you.

And two: the best kind of self-defence is to get the hell out of there.

Both lessons stayed with me.

I couldn't take this bastard down. No way.

But I could outrun him.

Anderson was built like a tank. Meaning he had the same weakness: power but no real manoeuvrability. That gave me the advantage.

He'd waited until this moment to confront me because there was no-one else around. He didn't want to make this public. Meaning my best hope was to head for other people.

Back the way I came.

I pushed off the safety barrier, bolted along the bridge. He followed me. I could sense him back there, no idea how close he was.

I wanted to look back. Knew I'd only slow myself down. I played some rugby in High School – member of the team for all of five minutes – but still there was something in the game that connected with me more than football. I wasn't the largest lad on the team, but give me the ball, I'd run like a bastard with it. The trick was not to watch who was behind you, but to keep barrelling through. Turn your head, you forced yourself to slow down. It was a matter of instinct as much as anything else. So what you did, you kept your eye on the line and you ran for it. To hell with whatever else was going on.

My right leg was beginning to ache. Every time my foot hit the path, shockwaves rattled up, as though my limbs couldn't cope with the stress.

But I couldn't slow down.

It wasn't –

Maybe Cal Anderson used to play on his school team, too. Maybe I'd skipped the part of his file that said he played for the force. Whatever, he caught me in a perfect tackle, Head low, grip on the knees rather than the waist, the idea being you stop the other guy kicking back and landing his studs in your face.

I barely felt the impact.

But I went down. Hard.

My hands came up. I twisted my face away from the impact.

It wasn't enough, of course.

The rough pavement scraped at my open palms. I roared in agony. My face caught fire down the left hand side.

Anderson rolled off me.

I tried to get up. Only managed to roll over onto my back. My breath came in short bursts. My throat threatened to close up, lungs ready to burst.

Cal clambered to his feet. No need to rush. I wasn't going anywhere.

One of those big boots swung at me.

Disoriented, I lifted my head to avoid the impact, wound up head-butting his steel toecap.

The world flashed into a blur of darkness.

On the inside of my skull, a drummer started on one hell of a solo.

More pain. Swift, sharp and calculated kicks. Anderson

spreading the impact. Each one fresh and raw.

Anderson's file had talked about "excessive force". I was getting a first-hand experience.

Soon enough, the pain started to fade, the force and the violence fading into the background. I felt strangely calm, almost as though I was adrift in the ocean. The pain seemed distant and oddly unreal, happening to someone else.

My eyes were closed.

Blood soaked through between my eyelids.

I just didn't care.

I just let it all drift away.

At some point I guess I passed out. Until I felt a hand cup the back of my head, lifting me up.

"Y'alright, pal?"

I don't know if I said anything.

At that point, my body just gave out.

My last thought was of Susan.

FIFTEEN

"I'm worried about Dad."

Susan was barely in the door. Her face was flushed, and her eyes looked watery. This was three months after Mary Furst. We weren't exactly living together, but Susan was round most evenings. I don't remember when she took a key; it had been a natural and unplanned occurrence, I guess.

We went through to the living room. She sat on the sofa. I stayed standing. Moved in front of the window. The sun was high, streamed through the glass, warmed my back through my shirt.

"You know anything else?" I asked. "About what happened."

Susan shook her head. She slipped off her shoes, and stretched. Tired. Frustrated. She said, "He won't talk about it. Mum's just saying the same thing over and over, that she can't take it any more."

Three days now. Her mum was moved out, settled in to her new place. Her dad was keeping the old house, rattling around in there by himself. He didn't say much when Susan went to visit. Given everything that had happened lately, that wasn't a surprise.

I just stayed back.

Kept my nose clean.

Figured all I could do was be there for Susan.

It's a funny thing. When parents split and the kids are young, you feel sorry for the kids because they have to be frightened and confused by the situation. But watching Susan, I realised it was just as tough when the kids were grown up, too.

I went to the kitchen, took a white wine from the fridge. Susan came through and smiled. I poured her a glass. She grinned and raised it as though in a toast.

"Your dad's going to be fine," I said.

"Can't blame him for being terse. Given everything that's..." she hesitated. We hadn't really talked about what she did for me. We'd spent months skipping around it. And now it was here, between us.

Hanging heavy.

Susan said, "Maybe I should go. Back home. Maybe this, maybe we..." She turned.

I didn't even think about it. Just reached out. My finger-tips brushing her elbow.

#

"Every time I see you, Mr McNee, it seems like someone has just handed you your arse on a plate."

I coughed.

My chest rattled. I thought something might dislodge, that I was going to cough up some part of me I didn't recognise but that was vital to my long-term health.

It didn't happen.

"You should invest in some training. I'm the patron of a boxing club in Lochee, if you ever fancied taking a round in the ropes."

I pulled in a breath, sat up and swung my legs off the ratty couch. Forcing my eyes to open as I did. The room was poorly lit. Couple of desk lamps. Wooden walls. A desk that had seen better days.

And behind the desk? The voice that had been talking to me?

Oh, aye.

How could it fail to be him?

Burns ground out his cigarette in the ashtray on the desk. He smiled at me, patiently, as though he'd been hanging around for a long time waiting for a response.

I said, "Would have been quicker to get me to the hospital." Not sure how long I'd been here. Or even where here was.

"How safe would you have been there?"

"What are you saying?"

"You know the prick who attacked you. What he is."

"A cop."

Burns smiled. Cold. Perfunctory. I don't know that I've ever seen the man smile genuinely. Not in my presence. There's always something else going on behind the façade. Maybe because of the life he's lived. He doesn't know any other way to be.

I knew Burns's story. He'd told me how he'd had to fight and claw for every inch on his way up, and how standard morality looked a lot different where he came from. Maybe all of that explained his past, but it didn't justify the things he had done in recent years. Maybe he got so used to certain ideals that they no longer seemed wrong to him. Some days I believed that he saw himself as a man who did what he did for all the right reasons. In his head, he was the hero of the piece. Maybe he thought of himself like some kind of Robin Hood figure; the naughty man who would be exonerated in the final pages.

What I knew for a fact about David Burns was that he had learned over the years to push his guilt away. Tuck it up in a deep, dark place where he could pretend it didn't even exist.

Maybe I had seen that part of him once before. Just a glimpse, a reminder of his humanity. It had been over a year ago, when he came to me and asked for help finding his god-daughter.

The same god-daughter who had killed a man.

The same god-daughter that Susan had lied to protect.

What did I say about morality?

What was right sometimes depends on the situation. But even that couldn't justify some of the things that Burns had done.

Neither of us had spoken for a long time. Like a stand-off, both of us daring the other to be the first to say anything. Burns was the one to break through first. He said, "You don't like me."

"I don't like what you stand for."

"Oh?"

"I know your public face. I know what you think you are. But I've seen what happens because of the drugs your boys sell, because of the debts people owe you, because of so many things you do without thinking, without caring."

He shook his head. "We're going to go through this again?"

"One day you might understand. One day it might penetrate that thick skull of yours. That what you do – what you are – is wrong."

If I got through to him at all, he acted like he didn't notice. He pulled out a packet of cigarettes. Held them out. "How are you feeling, by the way?"

Sore was the answer. My muscles ached. Turn the wrong way, I could feel the fabric of my clothes rub against open wounds, sticking to drying blood.

I touched my face, gingerly, with my left hand.

Burns withdrew the offer of the cigarettes.

I said, "How does it look?"

"You'll clean up." He sparked his own cig. Took a long draw. Looked satisfied as he blew out a dark plume of smoke.

My right hand was throbbing. Another old wound. Two years earlier, someone had stomped on my hands, broken those small bones. The doctors had told me I'd never regain a full range of motion. It got worse in the winter months.

On a small table beside the sofa where I'd been lying, there was a glass of water and two pills. I looked at them.

"Painkillers. Just codeine." Burns tapped ash from his cig into the ashtray. "I may take advantage of others' weakness, but I could never condone the use of drugs myself. Not for myself. Or anyone who works for me."

"I don't work for you."

He nodded.

I said, "But Ernie Bright did." The words had to be forced out. Like even saying them was an admission of a sickening truth that tainted every good memory I associated with the man.

Burns made a clucking sound. A mother hen impersonation. "Still harping on that, McNee? You don't get it, do you? He didn't work for me. We were... friends."

"He was a cop. A good one."

Burns shrugged. "Keep telling yourself that. The world isn't black and white, and I don't know how long you can keep fooling yourself that it is. That you're the good guy and I'm the bad one and that's all there is to it. Christ, I expected more of you, son." He finally stubbed out his cigarette. "I know Ernie's history. About the bad old days. How he was supposed to get close to me so the force could use my contacts. The idea back then being if you let certain big guns do what they want, the criminal world will police itself. Not that I appreciate the description, *criminal*."

"What would you prefer?"

"I'm a businessman. I supply services for which there is a demand. And don't go getting all high and bastarding mighty with me, either. You know the truths out there. Better than you care to admit."

My body was shaking now. I couldn't hold out much longer, grabbed up the pills and the water. Nearly choked them back up as soon as they were down.

"You're lucky my man found you," Burns said. "Or else you'd have ended up like the Detective Inspector."

"You mean that was an attempt to save me?"

Burns looked at me for a moment with the kind of expression normally reserved for the terminally idiotic. "You don't think Constable Anderson was working for me, do you?"

"It's not like you don't have a history of corrupting coppers."

He laughed, then. Long and hard. Best gag anyone had told him in a long time. I worried he might choke. Okay, so *worried* was the wrong word. More like… *hoped.*

When he calmed down, Burns said, "If I wanted you dead, McNee, that's where you'd be. Don't you realise by now… I like you. We have a connection, you and I."

Aye, he'd said as much before.

The idea still made me feel nauseous.

Burns continued, "I like you, despite what you say about me, what you think of what I do. Because you don't want to understand. Because you're frightened. So you take the moral high ground where I'm concerned. And that's fine. But I need you to understand, we share the same concerns. For example, your friend…"

I cut in, "Lindsay's not my friend."

"You've been pretty bloody pally the last few days."

"Necessity."

"I thought the incident between you was maybe forgotten."

"Laid aside."

Burns shook his head. "Is there anyone in this world you like, McNee? I'm surprised you have any friends at all. But how bloody magnanimous to work alongside a man you loathe. Professionalism. Nothing like it. You know Ernie was a professional. That's what was killing him. We were friends and he was still a copper. I sometimes wonder if that's why his wife left him."

I ignored the last sentence. It was deliberate jab; an attempt to wind me up. I had to keep myself in check around Burns. He was looking for a weak spot. I wasn't sure why, but it was all part of the games men like him play.

"In your case, there are no grey areas. I know you and Ernie grew up in the same circumstances, that you knew each other, however distantly, at school. And maybe that's why he was conflicted. But in the end, you made him more than conflicted. You compromised him completely. Men like you have no grey areas."

"Aye, that's it," said Burns. "I'm the bad guy. The black fucking hat. The villain with the sneer. Maybe I should grow a moustache so I could twirl it in public and let everyone know how bloody devious I am."

I said nothing. Still trying to figure why I was here. And where I was.

The office was sparsely decorated. Nothing on the walls. The desk itself was mostly bare except for the ashtray and Burns's smartphone. Aye, of course he needed one of those, being a "businessman" and all.

"You want to know what you're doing here," said Burns. "Aye, well, you've been given a wee brain shake there, so I guess I can forgive you for being slow on the uptake." He opened a drawer in the desk, pulled out a bottle of Grouse and two glasses. Grinned. "I thought the old soak would have something lying around. Hair of the dog and all."

I didn't ask the obvious question. He answered it anyway.

"Place belonged to a man who got in over his head. Oh, don't kid yourself, get on the fucking moral high horse. He knew what he was doing. It's not like I'm trolling the sheltered housing looking for the mentally retarded." As he spoke, he poured two glasses. When he was done, he pushed one of them across the desk towards me.

I kept quiet.

He'd get to the point in his own good time. Burns had an ego. Liked it to be massaged. One of the reasons why he surrounded himself with a certain type of thug. He was all about appearances and perceptions. Sure, he didn't care who did the dirty work, but he did give a toss about who he was seen with, how he was perceived by other people.

Why he liked to talk. Self-justification. Making sure other people see him the way he saw himself. I'd learned over the years that if you listened closely to what he said, sometimes you heard more than he wanted you to.

That was the problem with the ego. In the end, it was unconcerned with privacy.

"The man who owned this place was a gambler. Knew the risks. Liked them, in fact. The fear of losing, he got off on it. He was a junkie for risk. Just a pity he didn't like the reality of loss, that final, inevitable moment when the risk becomes real, when you finally have to pay. Poor bugger killed himself a couple of weeks ago. Sad incident. Plastic bag over the head and..." He pointed to the roof. "See that support beam, he wound up swinging from there. Electrical cord."

"And he left this place to you? He was a relative? A good friend?"

"He owed me this place. And all the money tied up here, too. It was a shame what happened, but..." He took a slug of the Grouse. Said, "But you don't care about some sadsack shitebag. You want to know about Cal Anderson."

"You said he's not one of yours."

"No, he's not. Matter of fact, he's working for a consortium of powerful men who would be perfectly happy if I were to suffer some kind of accident. Preferably the kind of accident that killed Ernie. You know, where at its very best it becomes death by misadventure."

"What do you know about Ernie's death?"

"I know that no-one who worked for me was involved. I also know that someone wanted Ernie's connection to me to become public knowledge. That they wanted men like you to be looking very closely at my connection to your precious Detective Inspector."

"Why?"

"It's a good question."

"Do you have an answer?"

Burns took another slug of his whisky. Pushed the other glass further across the table towards me. The gesture almost insistent. No-one likes to drink alone.

Which was why I ignored it.

Burns said, "We've been here before, but I hope you'll realise the opportunity I'm offering you. I was hoping to retain your services."

"You're right," I said. "We've already had this discussion."

"And even you can't be so bloody pig-headed to deny that we could have avoided a lot of trouble by working together in the past."

"Is this how you got Ernie? Sweet talk? Made him doubt himself? The choices he'd made?"

"I won't deny the man was conflicted," Burns said. "But the old bugger was never compromised. Not by me. Not like you think. I've told you before, sometimes you look at things the wrong way."

I thought about when I saw Ernie at Burns's house. Just over a year earlier, the image still burned in my memory as though it was only a few hours ago: my mentor standing in this gangster's back yard dressed in white chinos and holding a glass of wine like it was any other dinner party with any other middle class, middle-aged friend.

The shock was a brick to the back of the head. Worse than any beating I'd taken.

Betrayal is something that doesn't leave. The scars may not be visible, but they linger, and soon enough you're the only person aware of them. And you know that they won't ever leave no matter how much you try to ignore them.

Ernie had betrayed me. Betrayed his job. Betrayed the man I had believed him to be.

Was that his fault? Had I placed too much expectation on him?

I'd always believed Ernie Bright to be the model copper. The absolute ideal. I had held him to high, maybe even impossible standards.

Why? Because he had believed in me? More than that, but it was a good starting place. It was Ernie who'd got me the CID gig in the first place. He'd helped me out of uniform and onto the fast track.

"You're a natural detective," he'd told me once. "Too idealistic, aye. But that doesn't have to be a bad thing." Had he been trying to tell me something?

Burns brought me out of my memories. "The last few months, Ernie told me he couldn't take it any more, that he had to maintain a distance. That he was going to come after me hard if I dared step out of line. I think that was because you found out that he was..." Burns paused for a moment. Poured himself another whisky. Didn't offer me anything this time. As he screwed the lid back on the bottle, he finally seemed to have found the word he was searching for, "... fraternising. It's the old cliché, McNee. Me and him, under other circumstances, we might have been friends. We're the same age. We come from the same place. Grew up in the same streets."

"What made him different to you?"

"Luck." Burns shrugged. "What makes anyone different from anyone else? Christ, McNee, human beings are the most unpredictable creatures on the planet. Psychologists claim to know so much about what makes us tick but the truth is all they know is shite."

There was something we could agree on, at least. Some common ground. But still I had to wonder if he was telling me what I wanted to hear, playing some kind of game. My paranoia was on full tilt, and I wasn't sure if it was because I was still groggy after the beating or I was sensing a real deception on the part of this old man.

I said, "Who would want to frame him?"

"For one? That bastard who tried to kill you –"

"We don't know that –"

"He was trying to kill you." Burns spoke with a finality on the matter.

I realised that I hadn't asked what happened to Cal

Anderson. The implication was that one of Burns's boys had saved me.

The question was how?

Burns was a man who believed that old cliché of fighting fire with fire. Sean Connery in *The Untouchables*: *You send one of his men to the hospital, he sends one of yours to the morgue.* And in a strange way, I knew that Burns considered me one of his men.

He'd said it before, that he saw something of himself in me. I'd always thought of the statement as a kind of manipulation, trying to appeal to my ego. But I was beginning to wonder if he wasn't telling the truth. I'm not sure what frightened me more. The idea of his admiration. Or the idea that I deserved it.

"He was trying to kill you," Burns said. "Because you were close to the truth. You and Detective Inspector Lindsay." He waited for a second, as though expecting me to fill the silence. I didn't oblige, so he continued: "Your man Lindsay had three names. All under investigation themselves. All of them beat constables."

I gave him that one. "And not one of them looking at promotion," I said.

"And not one of them connected to Bright."

"Someone wanted him out of the way?"

"There's that brain," said Burns. "I always said you were a bright lad."

"Do you know who it is?"

"I have my suspicions."

"Then what do you want from me?"

"It would be easy to let myself get caught up in this. To rise to the bait. Because whoever's behind this, they're going to be coming after me. That's why they made it look like Ernie Bright was guilty. But trust me, I couldn't have pushed him into dealing or holding or anything like that. You have to know that men have limits. And Ernie made his clear."

He sounded paranoid. Desperate. A catch in his voice I'd

never heard before. He had always seemed so self-assured and absolutely confident in his own actions.

I figured there was something he wasn't telling me.

Something he already knew.

Men like Burns never tell anyone the whole truth.

"I'm asking you to do what you do best, McNee. Gather the evidence. Find the man responsible."

"And then?"

He smiled. Patiently.

I shook my head. "Not interested. Not for you."

"I have a name."

I stood up, grabbing at the desk for leverage. My body was still shaking. The codeine had dulled the pain a little, but not enough that I could function as normal. It took a lot of effort to remain on my feet. I could hear a noise like the sea heard through a shell.

I made for the door, each step slow and deliberate. Burns didn't move. Didn't try and stop me. He wasn't going to strong-arm me. He wanted to prove the point to me. Let me know that he wasn't just a criminal.

He would let me walk. But not without dangling some other bait.

As I put my hand on the doorhandle, he said, "Kevin Wood."

I turned. "What?"

"Just a name," he said. "But I can see you've made up your mind."

I nodded. The name sounded familiar, but my head was fogged and all I wanted to do was crawl into a dark space and go to sleep.

I could have stayed. Listened to what he had to say. Instead I thought, *sodit*, and opened the door.

Burns said nothing.

Just let me walk.

SIXTEEN

There was a taxi waiting for me outside. I couldn't have told you where we were, just an anonymous looking warehouse on the edge of a residential street I'd never seen or at least didn't recognise in the dark. The driver of the taxi was quiet, seemed to know where I wanted to head. Likely he'd been warned in advance. I checked my phone as we drove, saw a message from Susan.

Another follow-up an hour later. Both asking where I was.

I did the maths on how long I'd been out. Wondered how it must have looked, what Susan was thinking after seeing the way I left the ward back at Ninewells.

Light was beginning to lick the sky as we pulled up outside my building. I offered the driver cash, but he said it was all taken care of.

When I got into the apartment, I found Susan sitting in the living room, the lights off.

She said, "Where were you?" sounding accusatory.

Then she saw the state I was in.

"Jesus, Steed!"

#

I sipped at the coffee. My mouth hurt. There was the taste of blood. Thick. A gag reflex when I realised what the sensation was.

The coffee burned hotter than expected, maybe an exposed nerve somewhere in one of my back teeth. I tried not let it show. More than likely, I failed.

Susan sat across from me. "I thought you were past this."

"It's nothing."

"Crap it's nothing." She looked guilty, then, her eyes suddenly breaking contact. When she spoke again, her voice was softer. "What, you got upset, so you went looking for a fight?"

I shook my head.

"Steed, I know you. I remember what you were like after…"

"… After Elaine died. You can say it, Susan." But could she? Elaine's death was over three years ago, now, and still it came between us. Perhaps because of what happened all those years ago. One moment where Susan and I had reached to each other for comfort, wound up pushing each other further away.

That… mistake… still hung in the air, even though we both knew it was nothing to be ashamed of anymore. Still, both of us pretended it hadn't happened. Did that say something we couldn't express?

Being an investigator, much of your job is figuring out other people's motivations, seeing who they are and figuring why they do what they do. The thing you realise fast is that the most difficult people to figure out are those closest to you.

And yourself?

Forget it.

Susan faltered as she tried to continue speaking. She started to twist the skin on her left index finger as though she were playing with a ring. But she didn't wear much jewellery and certainly not on that finger. "After Elaine died… Steed, you were a mess. You were out there looking to die. You know that, don't you?"

The inside of my head felt thick, as though my brain was wrapped in a damp cloth. I put down the coffee, reached up to massage my temples.

Susan said, "I wanted to reach out to you. I didn't know how. Every time I tried, you were wrapped up in your grief and anger. You let them define you."

I wanted to stand up. Walk out.

But I didn't. Because she needed to say this. And I needed to hear it, too.

"Two years ago," Susan said, "I saw you like this. Your hand busted up. Your face split open. Jesus, someone had tried to shoot you, and you acted almost like you wished they'd succeeded."

I looked up. "Things are different now."

"Really?"

"I'm backing off. This is too big for me."

She said, "I've heard that before." But then she stood up, came over and put her arms around my shoulders, kissed the top of my head. The fleeting pressure of her lips on my scalp made me think of the sweep of a gentle breeze passing across me on a summer afternoon.

#

Later, in bed, Susan lay with her head on my chest. I stroked her hair. Said, "This is going to be a strange question. But did your dad know Kevin Wood?"

The name had been bubbling in my head for a while. Earlier, when Burns had tossed it at me, I had barely registered what he was saying.

Now, later, my mind calm, the pain a low background buzz, I realised why I knew the name.

Kevin Wood.

Deputy Chief Constable Kevin Wood

Second-top cop in Tayside. The man tipped for the top spot when the current boss left.

When she heard his name, Susan gave a little laugh. "I

guess… he was… Dad's… I guess you'd say Wood was his nemesis." She laughed the word off, as though it was ridiculous. As though in real life, no-one would dare use that word. Certainly, it had a melodramatic quality I was sure she didn't intend.

"There was bad blood?"

"He came up at the same time as Dad. Look, you know how you are with George Lindsay? Guess that was my dad and Kevin Wood. Serious hatred there. But with Wood, Christ he was a sleazeball. I met him a few times. Gave me the shivers just to shake his hand, you know?" She sat up, leaned on one elbow to look down at me.

I said, "I never met him. But from what I heard he was the Marmite of police officers."

"Don't know about Marmite. Even Lindsay used to call him…" She hesitated. Directly quoting her superior wasn't something she did with ease. Susan had no problems with swearing, but had never felt comfortable using the words herself. Except in those rare moments when her guard was down, when the pressure was on. Took a burst of willpower for her to get it out: "A power-grabbing cunty-baws."

"Makes what he calls me sound complimentary."

"Where'd you hear his name? I mean, Wood…"

"It's nothing."

She nodded. Tried to look relaxed, like everything was normal. But her body was tense, the doubt running through her in waves.

She was afraid. I didn't know if it was for me.

"Things are different," she said. "Things have changed."

"Yes," I said. "They have."

#

I woke early evening. Body clock screwed.

Susan was gone.

No note.

I went through to the shower, blasted the heat high and stood under water hot enough to scald. Twice I had to lean against the tiles to stop from toppling over.

All I'd been through, I was nearly knocked out by a jet of warm water.

When I was done, I looked at myself in the mirror.

The man who stared back looked tired.

Like he couldn't take the pace any more.

How long could you keep punishing yourself before you dropped?

SEVENTEEN

There was no-one in the ward from the force. They'd done their bit. Probably knew that Lindsay would get pissed off if they hung about too long, would want them back at the job.

A nurse allowed me into the small room where Lindsay was hooked up to a machine that controlled his breathing.

Induced coma.

Jesus.

I pulled up a chair. "Christ, so it's come to this, has it? You're my confidant. And only because you're in a coma and can't talk back? So consider this reason enough to get better. Because if you don't come round, I'll keep coming back to whine at you. Like the bawbag you keep saying I am."

There was no response, of course.

I kept talking: "I promised Susan I'd leave this alone. Same promise I make all the time. Aye, the same one I keep breaking. But I don't know if she understands why I can't walk away. Or maybe she does. Either way, I think she just wants to lay her dad to rest without dragging up any more ugliness. It would be easier. To brush all of this under the carpet."

I turned back to look at Lindsay. His chest moved up and down. The machine gurgled.

But he didn't move.

As though he was a simulacrum of the man I'd known; a fake, a stand-in.

I didn't know quite what to feel. The old animosity I'd come to rely on when dealing with Lindsay seemed petty. I found myself thinking about how he'd react if he knew what I was thinking. He'd be telling me what a screw-up I was. How I wasn't able to leave things alone. How I should just leave this to the bastarding professionals. The poor pricks like him who were paid to deal with all this shite and do it right.

He'd have a point, of course.

I'd done all I could. I needed to take what I had to the proper authorities. To Discipline and Complaints.

But I was hesitant to do that, a little voice at the back of my brain asking,

What do I have?

A name.

A rumour.

Sure, I had evidence on the three corrupt constables. But given Lindsay had already got information on them from D&C, my stepping forward would hardly be revelatory. And if anyone asked me about Cal Anderson, I couldn't really say what had happened to him. If he turned up dead, I'd just be putting myself in the shite.

I knew the truth about what had happened to Cal Anderson. Because, for all his talk, Burns was a man of swift, brutal and decisive action.

I wondered how long Anderson would be kept alive.

Whatever happened to Anderson, I was certain Burns wouldn't be present. Deniability was his watchword. The old bastard had become careful in his old age. Aside from whispering a few words in the right ears, he made sure to keep himself away from the scenes of the crime. That was why no-one had been able to touch him.

It doesn't matter, you pansy wee prick.

I looked at Lindsay. His eyes were still closed. He hadn't

moved. I'd just imagined what he would say. From this angle he looked small. Weak and insubstantial. His arms were pipe cleaners, his frame thinner than I recalled.

I heard a sound from the door. Turned and saw a woman there. Tall, with long mousy hair that fell in waves down her back. Dressed in blue jeans and a black polo-neck. Her eyes were large, making her look years younger than she was.

She said, "Who are you?"

"You're Mrs Lindsay?"

She nodded.

"I used to work with your husband."

She came into the room. "He'll recover. That's what they're saying, anyway. Doctors never give you absolutes. So I'm taking that as a good sign."

"I'm glad."

"You're CID? You look in pretty bad shape for a detective."

"I've had a bad day," I said. "And I'm not CID. I was. Once." I wondered, what did Lindsay tell his family about his working life? Did he tell them about the work he did? What he thought of his fellow officers? How much did his wife know about what he'd been working on before he was attacked?

I gave her my name.

Her eyebrows raised and she shook my hand. "Don't take this wrong, but you're the last person I would have expected to see."

"We had our disagreements," I said.

She smiled. "I often thought he had more respect for you than he admitted. He put so much time and energy into complaining about you."

"I never knew what I did to annoy him."

"I'm not sure he did either. He's funny that way, always has been."

She took the chair I had been sitting in. Reached out and took her husband's hand. Her grip was gentle, more a caress than anything else.

"I always understood," she said, "that he could be one person on the job and another at home. He feels a responsibility, I guess." She smiled, and I wished I could see the memories replaying in her head. "He was the same when we met..."

"Where did you – ?"

"University," she said. "My first year. He was shy, you know."

I nodded.

"I know he's all bluster at work," she said. "I've heard the way some of you speak about him. But he has to do that, you know, to be heard." She was trying to smile again, but it wasn't working. The tears were breaking through. "He's a sweetheart. You should see him with our son. I couldn't... I didn't want to bring Alan here. I don't know that... he's just turned seven, you know? He knows that Daddy's sick. He hopes he gets better. But I don't want him to..." She took a deep breath. "No-one will tell me why this happened."

"No-one knows," I said.

"I want to know."

"There are people working on it." Meaning the police, the proper authorities.

She said, "You?"

I said, "Yes," without even hesitating.

Realised once the word was out there that I couldn't go back on it.

That I didn't want to.

EIGHTEEN

We took a coffee in the reception. Standard vending machine fare; sour and unpleasant. Taste didn't matter, really. Holding the drinks gave us something to do.

"Did you ever meet a colleague of your husband's; a man named Kevin Wood?"

She laughed. At least I think it was a laugh. A sad little sound, halfway to a cry. "You mean the Deputy Chief Constable for Tayside?"

"Aye, that'll be the one."

"You know how much you annoyed George?"

"Probably the understatement of the year."

She shrugged, as though saying I didn't know what I was talking about. "Well, you were an annoyance, a pain in the arse... but he hated Kevin Wood. I mean seriously." She licked at her lips as though they were suddenly drying up. "You know they joined the force in the same year? Only difference was, Kevin liked to play politics. And maybe more."

"Corrupt?"

She shrugged. "I don't know. George never came out and said it, but then he didn't like to make baseless accusations." She smiled. "Maybe that sounds strange to you."

I thought of the insults he'd thrown my way down the years. Wondered if I could really deny any of them. He used to make me angry, spitting mad. But the truth will do that to you.

I said, "What about Ernie Bright?"

Her forehead creased. She said, "You know how upset George was when he heard about that man's death? I don't know that I've seen him take anything so hard."

When I was on the force, I remembered that at best Lindsay and Ernie Bright had maintained a professional relationship. But the tension between them had always been clear to those who cared to notice.

Ernie had once called it a "clash of personalities", and I think maybe he meant that sincerely. But you didn't have to like someone as a person to respect them as an officer. The world is more complex than that.

"I don't remember anything about the two of them." She shook her head. "After a while, if I'm honest, I forgot the details of what George used to say. Sometimes you just need someone to rant to. Not to remember everything you say to them." She looked at me strangely. "Are you married?"

I shook my head. "I was engaged."

She raised her free hand to her mouth. Gesture of shock. Eyes wide. "Oh God, I'm sorry. He told me and… you know he did everything he could to…?"

I didn't want to hear this. Didn't want to be reminded.

Mrs Lindsay lowered her hand. "When he told me, I wanted to… I don't know, I didn't know you and I felt so sorry for you."

When Elaine died, the worst part had been the sympathy. Words that became a blur of abstract senti-ment. People going through motions because they didn't know what else to do. That somehow hurt more than the memory, the fact that people were walking on eggshells around me, uncertain what to say, as though the slightest thing might set me off.

They meant well, of course.

Like Mrs Lindsay. She said she felt sorry for me. She didn't know me. Only knew what her husband had told her.

And what did he tell her? Did I even want to know?

I said, "It's in the past."

"He never told you what he found out. He said he didn't know –"

"He found nothing," I said, maybe a little too quickly.

Mrs Lindsay nodded, and her eyes darted to the coffee in her hand.

I said, "He thought Wood was on the take, then?"

"He said a lot of things," Mrs Lindsay said. "I don't recall specifics and I don't want to start saying things I don't know are true."

"I'm sorry," I said. "Forgive me."

"You look like you've been through tough times, too."

I stood up. Slow. Trembling a little. If she noticed, Lindsay's wife didn't mention it. Instead, she said, "When he wakes up, ask him about your fiancée. About what he found."

I said nothing.

Walked away.

#

In the car, I let my head batter back against the seat rest. I took deep breaths in and out.

The snow that had begun falling lightly the night before was back and was now falling harder. Heavier.

The temperature in the city had dropped. Below freezing. It was colder in the car than outside.

I turned the key. Blasted the heaters. Closed my eyes. I wanted to go to sleep. My breathing was unsteady, rhythms shot to hell. Every rise and fall of my chest was heavy.

I could have slept.

But for the residual adrenaline that kept me awake.

Kept me focussed.

Wondering where the hell I went from here.

NINETEEN

It was past ten when I pulled up outside Ernie's place. I'd slept for a while in the car, coming awake cold and tired. My skin was tender where it had bruised, and my mouth felt dry. But I was alive. And rested.

It was enough.

Ernie's house was empty. No lights. No movement.

I left the car on the street, made sure no-one was watching when I walked up the drive. I took the keys from my pocket. I'd taken Susan's spares earlier, knowing I'd be coming here sooner or later.

To look for leads. Or absolution.

Either one would do.

I opened the front door, moved to the alarm box. Part of me panicking suddenly, wondering if Ernie had changed the code. But he hadn't. It was still the same. Susan's birthday. Maybe not the most secure of codes, but memorable enough for both of the Brights to remember.

I stood in the main hall. Listened to the house. The silence.

Most places have a heartbeat. A background hum that you never really think about, but that's always there. This place didn't. It had died with the man who used to live here.

I stood there for a long time, barely drawing breath. As

though doing so would somehow insult Ernie's memory.

When I stepped forward, the creak of old floorboards was like an earthquake.

I closed my eyes for a moment. Half-expected to see Ernie standing down the other end of the hall when I opened them.

I used the light from my mobile screen as a torch, not wanting to touch the light switches.

Who was going to be looking here? Who was going to report a trespasser? Aye, so call it paranoia if you like. Sometimes you just know when something's wrong.

If I was a thriller writer, I'd say it was a gut feeling and act like that was a good thing. But it was merely instinct. And instinct is not always infallible. Just ask any good investigator.

On the upper landing, I moved down into the master bedroom. The bed was made up neatly as though expecting Ernie to return.

Through there again, a small back room: Ernie's office. Views across a conservatory extension, onto the back garden and down, out onto the river Tay. A faux-pine top desk by the window. The surface neat. Everything filed and squared away. A photograph of Susan as a child. Seven years old, smiling away on a farmyard, while a pig troughed about in the dirt behind her.

I checked the tray system. Nothing in the outbox. He was caught up, it seemed. Everything minimal and squared away.

I moved to the filing cabinet. The drawers were locked. I gave them a few good tugs just to be sure. They rattled loudly. It echoed through the empty house, sounding mournful.

In the books or the movies, I'd have been taught lock picking by a friendly criminal with a heart of gold. A good kid from the wrong side of the tracks. Fact was, I didn't know anyone like that. I could still go to work on some basic locks, sure. You pick up some skills on the force that you don't expect. But I wasn't equipped for something so small and fiddly. I could maybe open a poorly-designed front door if I had to, given time and space. But chances were I'd be caught before I had a chance to prove my skills.

I looked around the room. Saw the box on the window. Round, wooden, decorated with faded paintwork. I pulled off the lid. Inside, paperclips, old stubs, pen lids and...

Keys.

Small keys. Maybe five or six. No marks to show what they were.

The windows were double-glazed. Would take keys around the same size as the filing cabinet, I reckoned. Meaning I had choices. But also the time to make them.

I grabbed the keys, tried them one at a time.

Nothing. But they got the windows open. As much use as that was to me.

I felt a swelling in my chest. Old anger and frustration. Threatening to overwhelm me; make me lose control.

But I held on. Left the keys on the windowsill.

Looked around.

He wouldn't keep the keys on him. He'd keep them somewhere safe. Somewhere personal. Somewhere no-one else would look.

Where?

I figured he wouldn't want Susan or his wife to find it. But he'd need easy access.

I looked around the room. On the wall, framed photographs caught my eyes. Photographs of a younger Ernie. Official-looking. Taken on the steps of FHQ. I realised they were pictures of milestones in his career. His graduation from police college. His reassignment to CID. His promotion to DCI.

That last one caught me. He was with other men that I knew, all of them smiling, or trying their best to. Looking like they'd rather be getting on with the work they knew they had to do.

I reached for that last picture, took it off the wall. Felt

behind the frame.

Found the key in a small pocket down in the left-hand corner, a stitched on fold of paper you wouldn't notice at a casual glance.

I gave it a shot in the filing cabinet. Finally got that top drawer open.

The files inside were arranged and in a way I guess Ernie understood. Shorthand and initials that spoke of a personal system he either didn't want or need anyone else to understand.

Susan had told me that, growing up, her father's office had been a no-go area. She understood in no uncertain terms that it was *his* space. His sanctuary. He needed somewhere he could escape from the world, where he could consider things in seclusion without distractions. Or maybe he just didn't want his daughter to know the truth about the work he did.

How do you bring up a child when you know all the worst things that people are capable of doing to each other?

I took a deep breath, pulled out the files from the drawer.

Looked at the labels, trying to find some pattern.

K. Wood.

I pulled the folder, spread the contents out on the desk. Looking for some pattern. Unsure what that would turn out to be.

What I got were old newspaper clippings. Names and phrases highlighted in different colours. Maybe there was a code. Maybe he just couldn't find the same pen twice. The earliest clippings were dated 1971. Most of them concerned property developments within the city. Big deals to big companies. Certain names were ringed in red pen. The rings were loose, hurried. The red of the ink added to the impression of a scrawl made in anger.

David Burns popped up more than a few times. As a local businessman, of course. While his name was associated with much of the city's criminal activity, no paper dared print his name in that respect for fear of being sued. Or worse.

There were other names I recognised, too. Many of them wheelers and dealers, most with reputations that made you question their motives for doing anything. Only one name stood out to me; a prominent member of the local council: Peter Keller.

Keller was a Tory MP, younger than most of the other men in the articles which was why his name popped up later, still ringed with the same angry red circle Ernie had reserved for men like Burns and others who had come and gone from the landscape of Dundee's underworld.

One name, of course, seemed conspicuous in its absence.

Begging the question, why put these clippings in a folder marked *K. Wood*?

I put the articles to one side.

Found photocopies of old deeds and contracts. The copies were poor; a rush job as though whoever took the copies had done so with little thought for quality control.

Maybe worried they'd be caught.

I checked the names. Found a paper trail, every page signed by Wood.

Safety certificates.

Account transfers.

Purchases on land and business addresses.

Other documents I couldn't begin to understand.

There were bank details, too. Accounts Ernie couldn't have accessed legally. The documents all copies. Transfers and balances going back decades. The names changing. I was no financial expert, but I had a feeling many of the named accounts were placeholders. Diversions.

A noise from the other side of the house made me look up.

It came from outside. The front drive. The gritty crunch of a car on gravel.

I moved through to the bedroom, keeping low and in the shadows. Looked out the windows onto the drive, keeping my head down in case someone looked up and saw me.

Headlights arced through into the bedroom. I was careful to remain hidden, twisting my neck to get a good view.

The car was dark-coloured, in good condition. Might have been new. There were no tell-tale scuff marks, the bodywork reflecting ambient light. I couldn't see the plates. The engine noise was little more than a purr. It had been the crunching of its weight on the gravel that had alerted me. If Ernie had paved his drive, I might never have known anyone was there until it was too late.

Three men climbed out. Two from the front, one from the rear passenger door.

Dressed in dark clothes. Check their builds: bruisers, all of them.

Shite!

I ducked away from the window.

Maybe they were just making a house call. Well-built Jehovah's Witnesses. Or Mormons. They had a big presence in the city. Sometimes they tried to stop me in the city centre, tell me about God. I'd usually body-swerve them with the excuse that I just didn't have time for the Almighty. At that moment, though, I was ready to pray to Him.

I couldn't face a physical confrontation. My body still ached from my earlier encounter outside the hospital. It was only painkillers and sheer willpower that allowed me to keep on the move. The rush of adrenaline was going to help some, of course. I ducked down just beneath the sill and held my breath.

The men's feet crunched to the front door. Then stopped.

When they spoke, their voices floated up as deep, low rumbles. Native accents. Dundonians tend to have a unique pitch to their voice. It could knock down walls if anyone figured a way to control it.

The voices stopped. Just for a moment. Enough for the first bang on the door.

A unique sound. One you recognise if you've ever been on a drugs raid. The sound of a miniature battering ram lamping it against a heavy front door.

The training says:

Two thumps and in.

You don't fuck about.

Two thumps. Swearing. Footsteps downstairs.

Shite.

Even if they were on-the-level coppers here on legitimate business, it wasn't going to look good if they walked in on a local investigator indulging in a spot of recreational B&E. I had, from their point of view, no good reason to be here sneaking through a man's private papers.

Besides, Lindsay always wanted to be the one to send me down for something. And he'd be pissed off not to get the chance.

TWENTY

I had to move.

I could hear them downstairs. Angry tones rumbling up through the house.

Why were they here? Off their own back? On orders?

There were three coppers I already knew about under investigation. One of them was currently AWOL thanks to David Burns. But logic said there had to be more, that the rot went deeper than I could guess at.

If Discipline and Complaints didn't have anything on Wood, I had to wonder if he was the one who'd set up Ernie, who'd started the ball rolling on the events of the last few days.

Wood was corrupt. I had no doubt on that score. Not only did Ernie's paperwork point towards his suspicions concerning Wood's connections, but David Burns had flat out told me the man was corrupt. And inclined as I was not to believe a word that came out of the old bastard's mouth, I knew he rarely lied to me. Except through omission.

And he was good at omission, the wily old bastard.

In the office, I grabbed the keys from the wooden box. Went for the windows. Couldn't remember which of them I'd already tried.

First key fit but didn't turn. I tried the rest, forcing myself to work logically, keep my breathing and heart-rate down, stop my hands from shaking.

The voices were getting louder. So far no footsteps on the stairs. But I didn't have long. Whatever they were looking for, I had a feeling it was in the office. Sooner or later they'd figure that for themselves.

None of the keys worked.

Christ.

I heard footsteps on the stairs. Slow. Heavy.

Fuck!

One of these keys had to work on the windows.

Had to...

I quit fumbling with the keys, examined the lock more closely. Forcing myself to be thorough. One of my teachers at school had been like a walking cliché, but the one he used most was: *Less haste, less waste.*

Thank you, Mr Dow.

I examined the lock. Tried not to think about the bruisers downstairs. The hole for the key was in a small plastic protuberance for the handle. Like my own windows, you had to press the plastic in while you turned the key.

I acted fast. Second attempt, the window opened.

The big bastards were on the second floor, now. I could hear them in the hall just off the master bedroom. They weren't worried about being subtle. Guess they thought no-one was home.

"Fucksakes, man, this is a joke."

"You want to give him a call, tell him you can't be arsed?"

"Get to fuck."

An argument was good.

An argument wasted their time.

And gave me more.

I stuffed a few of the papers in my pockets. Didn't matter which papers they were. It would be enough to give me something to go on. I could fill in the blanks later.

I clambered onto the desk. Put too much weight on my

right hand. Couldn't hold my own weight. I fell, knocked over the filing trays and a pencil holder.

No way those bastards in the hall didn't hear.

I righted myself, taking care to use my left hand to take the weight. It was unnatural for me. I was a right-hander, so found my movements off balance and uncertain. Thing was, I needed to get this right or I would fall through sheet glass. The conservatory roof below was probably double-glazed, but that didn't meant I could just throw myself onto it.

I'd gone through enough this evening. Didn't know if this would be pushing it too far.

"Through there!"

They'd figured it out. Big didn't always mean dumb like in the films.

Bloody well wished it did, though.

I looked out at the drop again. My recently bruised skin seemed to pulse, trying to tell me this was a bad idea.

But it would be worse to wait for those big bastards to find me. I'd suffered bad enough with a beating from one man.

I went for it, trying to keep my weight spread even. Aiming for the structure's supports. Hoping they'd hold my weight.

I slipped down. Feet first. Slowed a little with friction. The last foot or so, I pushed against one of the solid supports and rolled. Off the edge.

Bloody stupid idea.

Could have been anything below.

Concrete. An abandoned mower.

What I hit was grass. Well maintained. A spring in the sod that served to lessen the impact. Not by much, though. I still got the wind knocked out of me. Couldn't move for a moment, as I tried to catch my breath.

Thinking?

Did I hear something break?

In my head, I pictured a rib snapping, the loose end

puncturing something. Maybe a lung.

But it was simple paranoia. I forced myself to roll over, get up and lean back against the conservatory.

Voices from above:

"Out the bastarding window!"

"Jesus shite!"

"Think it was a burglar?"

"Fucksakes, just our luck. Don't give a toss who it was, we can't afford to –"

"So get the fuck downstairs and find him. He fell off that, he's no got far. Unless he's... like that bastard, Superman."

I didn't have long. And I didn't feel like Superman. All the same, I urged my protesting legs to start working again. Stood up. My left leg protested, refusing to take my weight properly. Another old wound. Another pain in the arse.

Could I make it across the garden?

What choice did I have?

I pegged it across the lawn. Exposed and open. Stumbling more than running, spending as little time as possible putting weight on my right side. Heading for the bushes that formed a boundary between Ernie's house and next door's property. There used to be a weak spot there where next door's daughter used to crawl through when Ernie had a barbecue. The wee girl was nineteen now, no longer in the habit of sneaking through to get a free sausage from the soft-touch neighbours, but I had to figure the weak spot was still there.

I crashed through the bushes, into shadow, hoping I got away before those bastards saw where I'd gone. On the other side, I slowed down, suddenly aware there could be motion-activated lights out here. I sneaked round the side of the neighbour's house, hugging the wall. Made it to the street without incident. And only then allowed myself to breathe.

I limped to the car, trying to look casual, as though I was

just out for a night-time stroll. But I was feeling wary, wondering when and if anyone was going to see me. Waiting for the inevitable lamping I'd get if the three stooges back at Ernie's house managed to spot me.

How much pain can one man take before he just gives up?

The last few years, I'd taken my share of punishment. Some of it, I suppose, could have been avoided. Much of it was my own fault.

Much of it should have killed me.

Did that make me lucky? Some days I wasn't sure.

In the car, I switched on the engine, made myself drive at normal speeds. Like I was a resident off out for the evening.

If I'd been one of the three housebreakers, I wouldn't have been checking the street. I'd have been keeping a low profile. hoping all that had happened was I'd disturbed an opportunistic burglar who'd just been in the wrong place at the wrong time.

All the same I wasn't happy until I was at least six streets away, with nothing and no-one in the rear-view.

#

Burns had given me a number.

A mobile.

I knew it was a disposable. Or belonged to someone else. Someone whose relationship with the big man was deniable.

Unless panic was making him sloppy. This was one of the few times I hoped he hadn't made a mistake.

I parked down by Riverside, took out my mobile and keyed in the number. But didn't press send. Just sat there, staring at the illuminated screen.

Another car drew in to the small parking area. Parked a couple spaces away. Flashed its lights. I didn't return the signal. Ignored it. Knew what was happening. Didn't care.

All the same, someone got out of the car. Walked over. A weedy looking little pervert in his early thirties. His hair was slicked back and he had a kind of stuttering walk that spoke of nervousness. He rapped on the window.

I ignored him.

He rapped again.

I wound down.

He started straight in, voice too loud, body shaking. Anticipatory tremors. Wondering if he was doing the right thing coming here after dark. He said, "I don't know how it works. But that's my bird, back there." Jerking his head back to indicate a girl with bleached blonde hair who'd turned the other car's interior light on.

I said, "You got the wrong guy."

"They said that this was the spot to –"

"And I say get the fuck out!" I reined myself in, the words coming out just short of a snarl. All the same, the man reared back as though I'd snapped my teeth at his face; a rabid wolf when he'd been expecting a docile dog.

As he retreated, I said, "Count yourself lucky, pal. I could have been anyone. Next time wait for your fellow perverts to flash back!"

He had trouble starting the car, the engine stalling three times before he peeled off out the spot and back onto the Kingsway.

Another time I might have laughed.

But all I did was stare at that phone. At that number. Wondering if I was already in too deep. If I had already chosen the action I would take. If it was too late to turn back.

If it had been too late for a long time.

TWENTY-ONE

The meeting place was on the nose, but still made sense in a strange kind of way.

Burns had asked me to go to the warehouse where Ernie died.

Remnants of investigation – crime scene tape fluttering sadly in the wind, traces of fingerprint powder on the door handles – served as a reminder of what had happened here, along with the ends of half-smoked cigarettes and other human droppings.

But while the echoes remained, there was no longer any buzz around the place, no real sense of humanity. The building was quiet and deadly still. Where there once had been life, now there was nothing.

Even before Ernie's death, the warehouse had been abandoned and forlorn. Ignored for years, probably decades, by a city that had concentrated on expansion as though it meant the same as rejuvenation. Dundee's landscape had evolved with new riverfront properties springing up, bright and shiny, while so many old buildings off the travelled tourist tracks had been left to rot.

You'd almost think that some people wanted it that way.

Burns was waiting for me in the back of a BMW parked just outside the main doors.

His driver got out first and walked towards me. I met

him halfway. He was checking me out as he walked, his eyes focussed and alert. Fair enough. Give Burns his due on the paranoia front. If what he told me was true, he had more reasons than usual to be cautious.

I recognised the driver. His build made you understand what people meant when they said, *Brick Shithouse*. We'd tangled once or twice in the past. Meant he was trusted. From what little I knew of him, he was the strong, silent type. Just what a man like Burns needed.

I'd done some close security work, knew the Brick Shithouse wasn't a professional. But the kind of security a man like Burns required wasn't likely to be vetted by the SIA. Burns preferred his own style and his own people. He couldn't come to the professionals because they were bound by codes and rules that would prevent them doing what he wanted. So instead he hired the biggest bastard he could find and relied on intimidation to do most of the work.

I nodded a greeting to the Shithouse. He nodded back. As though we had a kind of unspoken kinship.

He moved to the back passenger door of the BMW. Opened it. Ushered. A smooth gesture, and I figured it was copied from the movies. He would be thinking, *this is how a heavy should act.*

I tried not to smile at the idea. Got in the back of the car.

As the door closed, Burns said, "Well?" twisting round from the passenger seat.

I handed him the papers across the divide. Said, "There's another name on some of these documents. Wonder if they mean anything to you."

He studied what I'd been able to grab. Smoothing out the creases in the paper from where I'd crumpled them in my pockets.

"Here's the thing," Burns said, "Kevin Wood was and always will be a cunt."

I didn't react.

"Even for a copper," Burns said, "he's a shitebag. Ernie

had old loyalties and old friendships that complicated his job. And, aye, he wasn't as lily-white as you and your wee girlfriend would have liked, but he knew who he was and what he was and there were lines he would never cross."

"Wood was different."

"I knew the bugger when he was a kid. Even called him a friend, once. And let me tell you, he frightens the piss out of me."

#

Kevin Harold Wood.

Born to Harold and Edwina in Kirkton during the late 1950s. An only child. Like the old joke goes, his mum and dad took one look at the ugly bugger and said, *no more.*

Maybe it wasn't a joke. Kevin Wood was a big kid with sticky-out ears and a bad case of the plukes that kicked in with puberty. Joke used to be that they based the character of Plug from *The Bash Street Kids* on Kevin Wood.

But the main difference between Kevin Wood and any cuddly kids' comic character was that Plug wouldn't break your nose for laughing at him. Plug wouldn't kick your arse just because he could. Wouldn't ask for your dinner money and then take it no matter what you said.

Aye, less Plug and more *thug.* In the proper sense of the word. Except Woods was more than just muscle and anger. He had brains, too. Quickly realised that brute force wasn't the answer to everything. He started to figure out how to get what he wanted without being caught. Woods could be ruthless. But he didn't have to be punished for it. At high school, he ran with a small crew who he relied on to do his dirty work. Letting them get in all the trouble, Woods concentrated on acing his exams. Because he wasn't the kind of thug who refused to listen to his mother, and Mrs Wood wanted her son to excel, to have another life than the one she and her husband found themselves living.

That ideal stuck with their son, of course. Kevin Wood was part of a generation who would finally have *opportunities*, so she kept telling him.

All of this, of course, was according to what I was told by David Burns. David Burns who, for a short while, ran with Wood and his crew until he saw opportunities elsewhere, realised the kind of game Wood was playing. The kind of game where everyone else loses.

"He used people. Chewed them up. Spat them out."

I'd heard, down the years, the same things said about Burns. Sometimes I'd been the one doing the talking. I had to wonder if men like him had any kind of self-awareness. If they could ever see themselves in the way that others did.

But according to Burns, Wood was different from most of the lads in their neighbourhood. Sure, they had a surfeit of hard men, of kids who knew they had to be tough to survive. But Wood was a true bastard. People feared him. "No just the other kids. The teachers, too."

Earmarked as a potential major player, he surprised everyone when he hit his teens by suddenly walking away from the life that called him.

"He had opportunities. He'd been noticed. Back then, Kennedy Senior was the man running things."

Kennedy had been old school. After serving in WWII, he came back home to find that the country didn't need him for anything any more. So he did the only thing he could, and continued fighting. Built up a life and reputation through hard graft and ruthless desperation. His sons were supposed to inherit an empire both legal and illegal, wound up grinding both into the ground and dying violent deaths due to bad choices. Burns had been one of their dad's inner circle, but split and went independent after the old man's death. The rumour mill often pointed at Burns as a major player in the brothers' eventual deaths. A rumour that was never proven, of course.

Back in the bad old days, Kennedy Sr. had offered Wood

a slice of his pie; knew that one way or another the ugly lad was going places. But Wood walked away from the offer. A move no-one expected. And no-one understood.

Rumours bubbled, as they always do. Maybe Wood was setting himself up to go into competition. Thought he could take down the old guard. It was the way of youth, Burns said, thinking they could do everything. In the end, people wondered was he just another eejit with an ego who thought things would be better if he was in charge.

But it seemed as though Wood really did walk away.

Wound up in college. University.

Kept his act clean. Became a respectable adult. At least, that was the way it looked to everyone. No more scams. No more violence. No more connections.

And then the move that gave some observers a heart attack.

The police force.

"It was one of those moves you thought, aye, it has to be a scam. If you remembered who he'd been as a boy, you were laughing. Either he'd gone insane, fallen off the edge, or else he was playing games. But the truth was he'd been out of the picture for a few years by then. Nothing came about connected to him. He wasn't in the game because he'd never really done more than dip a toe in the water. And for a while, I thought maybe he really had changed. That something had happened. A trauma, you'd call it. Something bad enough to scare him straight. To make him see where the life would lead." He shook his head. "But I should have known. His kind never really change."

In the 1970s, drugs became a major problem. The trade began a boom period that some might argue never really ended. Burns was in on the racket. Of course, he and his kind were a precursor to the NIMBY persuasion: if any of Burns's boys or anyone in his neighbourhood got hooked, he came down on them hard. As Burns said, "I never pressured anyone. Told my boys that the hard sell never worked. You don't create junkies. The addiction comes to them naturally. And if they're too weak to combat it, they don't deserve respect or help."

But as with any business, Burns faced competition. Competition that didn't share his sense of "morality" or his reservations about working with junkies. Competition that played dirty. Competition with an unfair advantage.

"The thing with bent coppers is that they're every bit as bad as a junkie," said Burns. "It's always in them, this bad centre, this rot they can't get rid of. They can't help themselves."

And the other thing about bent coppers: They play dirty. "Worse than any of us," said Burns. "Amoral shitebags with no idea when to draw that line. They don't like you, all they need to do is claim the law is on their side and they can fuck you up and down before you have time to realise what's happening."

As during his high school days, Wood kept himself clean, kept himself removed from any hint of wrongdoing.

"But he was responsible – more than anyone else – for what happened to this city. You remember the bad old days, McNee. When the industry was gone, when unemployment hit the roof, when the city was going to hell. When men like me stepped forward and tried to do something, anything to help a city that was in danger of imploding. Like I said, if you deal in drugs, if you deal in anything, you play fair and only sell to those stupid enough to buy without any other pressure."

Listening to Burns, I knew that he was rewriting his own history. His own policies. His own methods.

Self-delusion. Came naturally to men like Burns. There had to be where even he was unsure of which lies were even close to the truth.

But he had one thing right: Kevin Wood was more of a threat, more of a villain, than Burns.

It came down to which side you fell on. David Burns was a self-deluding psychotic arsehole who had ruined so many lives that I could only imagine the ledger on his conscience. But despite his continual protestations, he knew what he was, and the role that he played in the game. He fooled people only insofar as he wasn't going to be caught, arrested and punished for the things he had done.

Kevin Wood, on the other hand, was supposed to be one of the good guys. A copper. Supposed to protect ordinary citizens from men like Burns, the man who ensured that decent people were free to live their lives without fear or without threat. *The thin blue line.*

I knew the truth, of course: that the police were often forced to tread lightly, making difficult decisions in regards to process that sometimes the people would never understand. But there was always a line and if what Burns was telling was true, Kevin Wood had, for decades, been so far over he probably couldn't see it any more. It was a memory, something in the far distance, lost to the horizon.

What made it worse was, if Burns was to be believed, Kevin Wood had essentially been fucking the city for decades and no-one had batted an eyelid.

"So if you've known about him for so long," I asked, "why is he only making a move against you, now?"

Burns smiled. Opened the car door and made to get out, gesturing for me to follow him.

TWENTY-TWO

As the warehouse doors slid open, they made a low rumbling sound; an ominous, thunderous echo that caused me to involuntarily shiver.

Inside, the building was dark. Burns pulled a torch from inside his coat to illuminate the interior, but the light seemed comically inferior against the encroaching shadows. Somewhere up in the rafters, there was the flapping of wings.

Every small noise echoed.

Burns said, "If it came down to the wire, I have no doubt that Ernie Bright would have locked me away for good. He was a good policeman. An honest man." As he smiled in the backwash illumination of the torch, he took on a ghostly hue; the devil stepping out from the shadows to offer a deal for which the only price would be my soul.

"Don't patronise me," I said.

"Check the conduct records if you don't believe me. Your friend was clean as a whistle. Like I said, he was merely conflicted. But I had no hold on him. Not even a sentimental one."

"So how did he end up dead? Why was he a guest at your house?"

"Over the last few years he had been asking about Wood. Trying to find out what I knew. He was onto Wood's game. While it's possible for a man to change, in the case of a man like Wood someone's always going to have suspicions."

We walked into the warehouse. Our footsteps echoed in the air around us. The torch illuminated the dust on the floor and floating in the air.

"Your man Ernie had come to notice little things about his colleague. I got the impression they'd never been friends, but something finally put Ernie's nose out of joint..."

Was this the whole truth? Burns's sins were often those of omission and I was coming to realise that he would only ever tell me as much as he needed to in order to ensure my complicity.

"You're saying that Ernie had a grudge against Wood? That was why he came to you?"

"More than that. Ernie was the kind of cop who needed proof, evidence. He was by-the-book. You know that, even if you came to doubt yourself. He'd seen irregularities that tracked back to Wood. He knew the man had a past and did some digging."

"And you helped him?"

"He came to me. Because it was mutually beneficial. Remember we worked together in the old days."

Ernie used to say the attempt by the police to work with men like Burns was the worst idea he'd witnessed in all his years of policing.

But he'd done what he was told. Because he was a good copper. Because he had trusted that someone, somewhere had a plan.

Hard to think of him as ever being that innocent.

"There were problems, of course. The more I told him about Wood –"

"– the more you told him about yourself."

Burns made a little noise from the back of his throat that I guessed was an agreement. "No-one likes a grass, McNee. Not on our side. Not on... theirs." I figured he'd been about to say *yours*, but stopped himself at the last moment.

And he was right to do so.

What was I any more? An ex-cop, sure. And most of the time I guess I still sided with them. Morally speaking, at least.

But I'd done things over the last few years that were at best ethically ambiguous. And I'd dragged other people – like Susan – down with me.

If I stopped to think about it, I don't know if I could really say what I was.

Maybe there are no heroes in the world. No good. No evil. No black hats. No white hats. Just people who make decisions, right or wrong. The only lines drawn are artificial ones, created through some desperate need to make sense of the world, to mark out behaviour and attitude in a way that is easily categorised.

We walked up a set of metal stairs, onto a gantry that ran across the perimeter of the warehouse. Burns told me what he knew about Ernie's death. "You want to know why he died? He died to send a message, McNee. He died because he was getting close to Wood, maybe had started flirting with your beloved Independent Police Complaints Commission or just put the man on notice. I don't know, but I know that he wouldn't be dead if Wood didn't see him as a threat."

Burns seemed to be taking Ernie's death as personally as I had. Or maybe I was just projecting. Looking for an ally where I was afraid I had none.

We hit the upper gantry.

"How's his daughter taking it? You and she are close."

He was vague about the exact nature of my relationship with Susan, as though uncertain what the situation was. Which made two of us.

"She's taking it hard," I said. "Her father's dead. His reputation has been brought into question..."

"And now one of her friends is in hospital and you, McNee,

144

her… whatever you are… you're nowhere to be found."

I could have lamped him. Instead, I bit back some retort about how he was to blame, how he was the one who had brought me here. How none of this would be happening if he hadn't stuck his fucking oar in. But he had me,

Because the truth was I had no idea how to comfort someone in grief. All I knew was what I was doing; following a trail of tragedy to its source. That's not the official job description of an investigator, of course. In my case, however, it was as close to the truth of the matter as anyone was likely to get.

Burns said, "You're a marked man, now. You know that Lindsay was supposed to be dead, aye? That they'll be sending someone after him?"

I nodded.

"I have someone at the hospital," Burns said. "The police – the ones that aren't in Wood's pocket – they don't know what's going on. And our man has enough influence that he can send any official investigation into a tailspin." He was turned away, but I imagined he was smiling when he said, "Looks like you have no-one to turn to but me."

I said nothing. We kept walking.

Our footsteps echoed. But now I was aware of another sound. Somewhere close by. Movement. Not birds or even rats. Something big.

Another person?

Burns shone the light along the walkway. At the far end, against the wall, I could just make out the hunched-over shape of a man. A big man. Chained to a pipe that ran down the wall. He had been beaten, and when the light fell on him, he turned his head as though he could escape it.

But there was nowhere he could hide.

Burns said, to me, "Recognise this prick?"

I stepped forward. Burns shone the light around me. I knelt beside the man. He looked me in the eyes.

I fought the urge to recoil. Remained calm. Yes, I recognised him. "Cal Anderson."

"He's been here for a few hours, now," said Burns. "Not really a chatterbox."

"Get," said the man, carefully enunciating as best he could through the blood he was still swallowing and the broken teeth, "to fuck."

I remembered an old joke about a man in a bar who says that swearing is the first fucking sign of a tired mind. When his friend asks him what the second sign is, the first man punches him out.

I stood up, "But he's told you about Wood."

"Loyalty," said Burns, "is unusual among shitebags like this one. But so far he's kept schtum. Maybe he's not such a bad person after all." Anderson responded to this with a snort. Spat onto the metal grille of the walkway. Burns said "Then again..." He looked directly at me. "This man is shite. Shite that should be shovelled off the pavements. Taken away so that decent people don't have to deal with it."

I said, "What you do is you turn him over –"

"Don't you get it yet, McNee? If we turn him over, Wood's going to make any charges disappear. This pathetic little bawbag's going to get a free ride."

"No," I said. "If you turn him over to the right people, then..."

Burns shook his head. "I thought you of all people would have got it by now, McNee, that justice isn't about law and order. That sometimes you have to bypass all these fucking rules and regulations because it's just the right thing to do."

He stepped closer to me.

I didn't step back.

"I know you know that, McNee. Because we're alike, you and I. You just need to accept it."

Burns pushed past me. Knelt down beside Cal Anderson. The other man spat at Burns's face, but it was a pathetic attempt, as though he had no liquid left. Burns stood up, wiped at his face with a sleeve. "Anger management issues. Christ, but he deserves whatever happens to him. He's told us all he can."

"So why show him to me?"

"To let you know that he was still alive. Because I know what happened after the death of your fiancée. You never found the bastard who was responsible. That must have hurt, maybe worse than losing her."

I wanted to walk away. But I stood there, gripping the handrail, listening to my heart beating. Loud enough that Burns and Cal Anderson must have been hearing it, too.

"Two years ago," said Burns, "You killed a man and stopped short of killing another. I know the rage you carried then."

I said, "I got over it." Sounding too glib, even in my own ears.

"No-one gets past that kind of anger, McNee. No-one. You know about my mother, don't you? That she died at fifty-five in an arranged accident. That a man I thought was my friend arranged to have her killed just to show me that he was willing to go further than he thought I ever would. The most satisfying day of my life was the day I killed him. Personally."

"And did that help?"

"Of course it fucking didn't. What, you expect miracles from life? But it helped channel my rage."

I said, "Forget it," knowing what he wanted me to do. In his mind, this was some kind of loyalty pledge. He was initiating me. Or attempting to.

He said, "You can't walk away."

"Watch me."

The further away from him I walked, the darker the warehouse became. My eyes struggled to adjust and all I could see were half-shapes and darker shadows.

Carefully, I picked my way down the stairs. My eyes adjusted enough to see where the exit was. At the bottom of the stairs, I walked more confidently towards the door.

Heard movement from the walkway above.

A roar cut short.

I don't know if I was aware of movement or if it was a self-preservation instinct. Either way, I stopped, and looked up. Saw something was dropping from above. An impossibly heavy shadow.

I stepped back. Something crashed to the floor in front of me. A sharp crack was audible beneath a sound like someone smashing a jelly with a hammer.

Light shone from above.

I looked at Cal Anderson's corpse.

His neck was broken, his head twisted so that his dead eyes stared up at me. If I was paranoid, I might have seen an accusation in them. But there was nothing there. No emotion. No life.

If anything, that made me feel more disturbed than blame or hatred.

Burns spoke, his voice echoing, bouncing off the inside of the empty warehouse. Seeming to come from every direction. "You have to find the strength to do what needs to be done, McNee. Or the world will get you. I know you have it in you. I've seen it."

I could have come back at him with something.

But instead I stepped over the corpse that lay in front of me and walked outside. I went to my car, got inside and started the engine.

No destination in mind.

All I wanted was to get the bloody hell out of there.

TWENTY-THREE

Susan was at the flat when I returned. She knew something was wrong. There was no point lying. Told her what I could. We sat in the front room, separate seats, facing each other. The setup was combative, but I was unsure if she even realised that. Rain battered against the window.

It was past two in the morning.

I went through the story, through what I knew, as best I could. She didn't stop me. Didn't even seem to react. Just listened to the story, face set in neutral.

There were things I didn't tell her, like Burns offering me Cal Anderson's life. Or what finally happened to the corrupt bastard. I guess Susan assumed, as I had, that Anderson was dead from the moment Burns's thugs laid into him.

Looking back, I can't say precisely why I didn't tell her. Other than to admit to what had happened would somehow make me complicit. Over years of talking to people, getting their stories, making narratives of their lives that would fit reports or case-notes, I found that so many would change their stories to make themselves look somehow better. Often omission wasn't even conscious, as though it was simply part of human nature to lie, dissemble and falsely remember the truth.

When I was done, Susan said, "You don't remember meeting Wood, do you?"

I hesitated. "I'd remember." And I would. I was sure of it.

"No," she said. "You don't. But that's okay. You were too busy trying to behave like a normal human being at the time."

#

A long time ago.

Longer than I cared to remember.

I had been the golden boy. Hard to believe, even though I was there. Detective Sergeant Ernie Bright had taken me under his wing. Told me I was a natural copper, but he wanted to teach me more than the mechanics of policing. To get ahead, he said, a really good police nab needs to play the political game. Which is how I wound up at a party, *chez* Bright, feeling awkward and out of place.

Elaine had been out of town. Had assured me that if I was my charming self, I'd fit in. I didn't need her to make me seem human. I could manage it for one night.

She had faith in me. More faith, even, than the man who wanted me to play the game.

My charming self, of course, had other ideas.

Lucky for me that someone else at the party wanted me to fit in. If only because her father's judgement and reputation was resting on how all the high heedjuns in attendance took to me.

Susan Bright introduced herself by scolding me for my behaviour. Over a few shared cigs in the back garden, she told me that if I didn't sharpen up and play the game she was going to kick my arse personally.

Sure, she was small, but she was tough. I got the impression she'd follow through on the threat.

The rest of the evening became a blur. Forced smiles and handshakes. The agony of small talk and political niceties; saying the right things to the right people. The trick, apparently, was never to agree but never to disagree either. I found that making odd noises to show that you were listening, and occasionally repeating what someone just said seemed to work.

I also made sure I had the same glass of wine in my hand for most of the night. Meaning that by the end of the evening, I was parched.

At one point, Ernie shepherded me into a gathering of CID detectives who were discussing a particularly chilling case that had captured the attention of the local press. A woman's body found out in the woods to the north of the city; mutilated and abandoned. They were finding themselves at a loss for leads after the most promising had petered out due to an oversight regarding the man's access to a vehicle for transporting the body.

One of the men had been tall and thin; you might have got papercuts if you accidentally brushed against him in the hall. He had big ears and eyes best described as bug-like. His skin was swarthy, pocked from teenage battles with acne that had left him looking leathery. This man had been leading the conversation and when he turned his attention to me, he seemed surprised and disappointed. It was the bug-eyes gave the game away: *why am I talking to this man? Who is he?*

All the same, he introduced himself: "Kevin Wood." His voice was oily and his over-friendly tones forced. I remember thinking that he sounded afraid of his own voice; working hard to control his natural accent. What came out was not quite RP, but just close enough to be false. At that time, Wood had only just been put in charge of CID operations in and around the city, and Ernie had whispered as we walked across that here was a man worth knowing politically.

All the same, I got the impression that on a more personal level, Ernie despised him. At that time, I didn't press farther, but I guess even by that stage Ernie had realised that the ugly bastard wasn't quite the supercop he had built his reputation on.

I think I suggested a few investigative ideas based on

what I knew of the case. Thinking that at the very least they'd say they already thought of them. But I needed to say something in order to join the conversation. Fresh voices and all that.

Wood sneered at me, and shook his head as though I was a particularly remedial kind of student. "It's not worth it," he said. "This case will be solved by detective work. Not by beat constables and their procedural ideas."

It wasn't what you'd call a glowing encounter. But I figured I'd done well by not telling him to fuck off. Or even lamping him one.

It was only one of several encounters that evening, and to be honest most of them hadn't gone as well as I or my mentor had hoped. Schmoozing, it seemed, wasn't my style. So I'd pretty much pushed my meeting with Wood to the back of my mind. Just one more arsehole among an evening's worth.

No-one worth bothering about.

#

"Dad always said to watch out for Wood. Never went into specifics, though. Just always said that he didn't trust the man. Felt Wood was up to something. He could just never say what."

The way Ernie operated was simple; he never advanced an idea without proof. While he believed in his gut, he knew that he always needed to back it up with proof. He had to know absolutely that he was right before he made a move. Which explained the filing system I'd found in his office; he'd been gathering evidence. I wished I'd had more time to go through them, but by now I knew the three men who'd arrived after me would have cleared – destroyed, more than likely – anything incriminating.

I said, "Your dad was building a case against Wood."

"Working with D&C?"

I didn't know for sure. "It's possible. Or else he was

getting ready to approach them." I was reluctant to offer any definitive suggestions. Feeling confused, wondering how well I'd ever really known Ernie Bright.

People are complex. Sometimes those we think we know best are the ones we know least. We have trouble talking about motivation because no matter what we tell ourselves, we never knew anything about the way they thought, how they viewed the world.

I had believed Ernie was the perfect copper.

Then I had been convinced that he was a turncoat.

And now David Burns – a man I had vowed never to trust – was telling me that Ernie had merely been conflicted, caught between personal feelings and professional obligations.

Like I said: *complex.*

I stood up and walked to the window. Looked out at the rain. Something about rain on glass, the way it slides down, splintering your view of the world outside, has always been strangely comforting to me. "I told you about your dad, about seeing him at David Burns's house."

"I couldn't talk to him about it. I wanted to. But then everything went to hell... and now..." She didn't finish the sentence. She couldn't.

Susan Bright was tough. Always had been. Had a reputation as a terror in the interview room. Hard men broke down when she turned her anger on them. She could walk into a room and people would think: *This is not a person I want to mess with.*

She was confident. In control.

Always.

Even over the last few days, despite a few wobbles, she had been holding it together. But her confidence couldn't last forever under the strain of the last few months. The last few days in particular. Sooner or later something would have to give.

Grief affects people in different ways. After Elaine's death the force asked me to see a psychologist. I refused, until they made me go following the incident with Lindsay. I lasted only a few sessions before walking out. But some moments stuck with me.

He had talked to me about grieving. How some people lash out. Some people internalise. And some people do both.

When it comes out – and, he told me, it always does – sometimes the people closest to you are the most surprised by the form it takes. You can't predict how anyone is going to grieve. Can't put a timescale on it. You can only watch and do your best to accommodate the person, try and help them move through what they need to do to get past the trauma.

I had no idea what to expect from Susan. She was always in control. What happened when she lost that?

I said, "Let's say he found enough that he was taking his evidence forward. Let's say that he was using his connection with Burns to try and gain more evidence. Burns keeps saying that he and Ernie were friends, that Ernie was conflicted. What if that wasn't true? What if your dad was just doing what any good investigator would do, using contacts to get at the truth?"

Susan nodded.

Not sure if she was buying.

Not sure if I was buying it.

But it was what we had to go on. And it made me feel easier about the past few years. Made me feel as though I wasn't so wrong about everything I had ever believed.

#

Two months after Susan admitted to killing the psychopath Wickes in self-defence, I popped into the Phoenix for a quick pint after the office was closed up. Figured I deserved it. Something to wind down after a long day crunching data and getting nowhere fast on an inheritance gig that looked like a dead end.

Ernie was there. At the far end of the bar.

The end-of-work crowd had finished their pints, and the bar was in the lull that comes just before the early evening rush. It was a time of evening I loved. Quiet enough that you could drink in peace, alone with your thoughts, if you wanted to.

The lad with long hair pulled my pint with some chat about how he enjoyed this time of night, before it got too mental. I paid up and then slid down the bar.

Ernie said, "I don't want to talk to you."

"Because of Susan? Or because of what I know?"

He shook his head. "You're a smart lad. Always have been. But this time you're seeing things that aren't there." He stared hard at his pint. "Not looking hard enough."

"So tell me," I said, "what it is I'm not seeing."

He tried to ignore me.

At the other end of the bar, the young lad looked at us as he cleaned glasses. Sensing the tension. Maybe trying to figure if we were going to make trouble. The Phoenix wasn't the kind of pub you found trouble. Any hint, the staff were quick on the alert.

I said, "You were at his house. You were drinking his wine. A guest, Ernie. Like the two of you were old friends. And, you know, I get it that you were his liaison in the bad old days when the brass thought they could make nice with the major players. Maybe during that time some lines got blurred, but you have to know –"

"I don't have to know anything, McNee. And neither do you. For God's sake, just leave me alone. You're a good man, and I used to have hopes for where you'd be going. But now... now, all I want is that you take care of my daughter. Not just because she sees something in you, but because I know this investigation into her conduct has something to do with you. More than either of you are saying."

I couldn't hit back at that.

Susan had lied to cover for me.

And every day, that was the first thing to hit me when I woke up. This strange feeling that I was a coward for hiding behind Susan's lies. But if I'd stepped forward, I suspect things would have been worse.

Her lie wasn't to protect me. It was to protect an innocent girl. We'd agreed that I should be the one to take the fall. And then Susan made her "confession". Knocked me off guard.

We still hadn't talked about it. Sex had become something that stopped us from thinking about consequences. It had always been between us, and now it was driving us further apart than we'd been before.

I said, "She knows about you and Burns."

"You told her?"

"She worked it out."

He nodded. Smiling? His head was half-turned away so he didn't have to look at me and so that I couldn't look at him. "Smart lassie, my girl. Never could hide much from her. Takes after her mother."

Did his wife know?

I said, "You know you can't be friends with a man like that. Even if you like him, Ernie, it's a professional –"

"Don't talk to me about professional, McNee," he said, keeping his voice calm. Knowing that people had noticed us. "Don't say a bloody word about it. Because if anyone here's a screw-up, it's you. Assaulting a senior officer like that? Christ sakes, he was trying to help you too. And we all had sympathy for you then, but look at what you became. Look at the chaos that always follows in your wake." He shook his head.

I thought about saying something else.

Realised I'd said too much.

Slipped off the barstool and walked away. Leaving my pint untouched.

A moment of self-control. But I never felt much pride about it.

Had Ernie Bright been trying to tell me something? Sounding conflicted because he couldn't tell me that the real reason he was getting close to Burns was so that he could get more information on Kevin Wood?

He had said it outright: I wasn't looking at things the right way. That there were aspects I couldn't see to the situation.

Months later, I had a kind of clarity. But it was too late to do anything about it.

Ernie was dead. And his own colleagues suspected – whether they voiced it or not – that he'd been dirty. They were the same fears I'd been harbouring for months. For the same reasons: they didn't have access to all the facts.

Sure, I could go forward, same way Ernie had been planning to. But given my reception at the hospital the previous evening, I doubted whether I could really convince anyone of anything. Ernie had been my cheerleader on the force following my exit from the Job, and now he was gone. Even Lindsay, who might have stood up for me in this case, was at death's door himself.

Unlike Ernie, I didn't have any concrete evidence and anything I had hoped to find would be long gone by now. It would be my word against those of fellow boys in blue.

Tell me who you'd believe.

And I couldn't help but think about Ernie accusing me in a moment of uncharacteristic anger of all the shite that follows in my wake.

He'd been right, of course.

It was my own form of self-delusion, this idea that I was doing the right thing when in fact what I did more often than not was fuck everything up. Maybe not a conscious decision, but unconsciously you'd think I could see the consequences of my own actions.

I was thinking about this when Susan said, "Wood knew that my father was getting close to him. Dad didn't think anyone would take his side if he went public with what he knew. So who's going to believe us?"

I didn't know. I walked over to her, put my arms around her. She pressed against me, raised her head so that her lips were at my ear. "I want him dead," she said.

I held her tighter.

They were just words. Uttered in a moment of despair. Just words.

TWENTY-FOUR

We couldn't just accuse Wood of corruption. It would become a game of his word against ours. And he would win. He hadn't played the game so long to suddenly get sloppy. We couldn't just rush in, metaphorical guns blazing.

In the back of my mind, I rolled Susan's words over and over.

I want him dead.

It was the kind of thing someone says without thinking. A moment of anger that would pass and give way to rationality.

This was Susan, after all.

How many times had she pulled me back from the brink?

What we needed was evidence. Or a reliable witness.

The sheets of paper I had grabbed from Ernie's place had one key name mentioned over and over again. A name I was convinced would be the weak link in Wood's chain.

Susan said she would stay out of it. Any action she took in the matter could affect the outcome of her hearing. She was already in enough trouble.

I said, "I'm sorry I thought that Ernie was– "

She shook her head, kissed me on the lips. It was fleeting and felt cold, oddly distant. When she pulled back,

I had to suppress a shiver. This sensation, the one my gran used to describe as "someone dancing on my grave".

She said, "It's okay. He was my dad, but he was only human. And one thing you learn fast in the police is that anyone's capable of anything." She tucked a loose strand of hair behind her ear. "I'll be fine. I just can't take any stupid risks."

I nodded.

She said, "And neither can you."

"I'm just going to talk to him," I said. "Persuade him to do the right thing."

As I walked out the flat, I found myself shivering again. Something was gnawing at the back of my skull; a half-formed idea or suspicion. A notion that something was very wrong, and that I was an idiot if I couldn't work out what it was.

#

My head was becoming increasingly fuzzy. The shakes were coming on: my left leg seizing up. My right hand was numb. I had to keep stretching my fingers out in order to get any feeling back.

What the hell was I thinking? These last few days I'd been pushing the limits. Which would have been fine if I was an action hero in a Hollywood movie. But in real life when you get battered about, it tends to have consequences. And not all of them are immediately obvious.

I drove carefully, sitting forward, forcing my eyes open. I could feel the car slipping along the road, this terrible sensation that I was about to lose control. One moment of distraction, I'd hit something or just plough onto the pavement.

Blame it on the lack of sleep. And maybe too many pills. Self-medication is a tricky business. A friend of mine, his brother had started medicating with over-the-counter painkillers, wound up just as fucked as any dope addict. Maybe worse.

I figured I was on the right side. That this was an unusual situation. All the same, part of me was panicking, struggling to stay sharp.

I forced myself to keep awake more through sheer willpower than anything else. Focussing on the goal, the end game. Knowing that once I was finished, I could let myself go. But I couldn't stop before I was finished. I knew that much.

The rain was heavy again. The windscreen was streaked. The lights outside became trails of orange and white that fritzed and sparked.

I kept my mind focussed.

On the road.

On the goal.

On the man I needed to talk to.

The man who would give me what I needed.

My eyes flicked between the road and the dashboard. The digital clock read-out:

03:37

03:38

03:39

#

Peter Keller.

Tory candidate, Dundee East. An influential man.

Sure, the Tories rarely got a look-in when it came to Dundee – we're a city of workers, traditionally Labour voters, even during the 2010 elections when people had lost faith in the "worker's party" that had so long ago discarded its own roots and ideals – but Keller was a man of wealth and property who still had a strong voice in local Government. He could easily bend the ear of the right people if there was something he really wanted.

What you'd call a good man to have on your side.

Look at what Ernie had gathered, you had Keller approving so many projects and initiatives that benefited

Wood and his various fronts, that you'd have to be missing your eyes and at least half your brain to not think Keller had been bought in some fashion. And was being kept. A good little pet.

When I pulled up outside Keller's house – a Victorian structure set back from the main road behind a walled garden and large trees – I noticed another car parked there.

Looked familiar. It had only been a few hours since I'd been sitting in the back, passing crumpled papers to the man in the passenger seat and feeling like I was crossing a personal line, hoping it was for all the right reasons.

I walked through the iron gate set in the boundary wall. Simple lock, no need for a key. The stone steps that led to the front garden were uneven with age; original features, probably something he was proud of.

The front garden was mostly grass. There a few neatly trimmed bushes and flowers arranged in a deliberate fashion. It wasn't a garden you took pride in looking after yourself. It was a garden you paid for.

I followed the path that bisected the lawn. Flat paving stones, evenly laid. The covered porch in front looked new. Probably called it a conservatory and paid three times the price. Double-glazed and so clean inside you had to wonder if anyone ever used it. Even the furniture facing out towards the garden didn't look as though anyone had ever actually sat on it.

There were lights on inside.

This early in the morning? Confirmed my suspicions about the car up front. Made me wonder if I was too late.

I rang the doorbell. Waited.

I wasn't surprised by the man who answered the door. Simply said, "Let me talk to him."

The thug – still awkward in the suit that Burns insisted he wore – stepped aside.

I think maybe he was smiling. But I couldn't really be sure.

162

Keller was on the sofa, his head tilted back, hankie pressed against his nose to stem the gush of blood. He looked out of shape; the kind of man who doesn't exercise, doesn't realise his lifestyle's catching up on him until he hits middle age and that spread just *happens*.

Burns sat in a comfortable armchair across from the politician. He'd helped himself to a glass of whisky. Or maybe he'd brought more of his own. Either way, he wasn't drinking so much as just sloshing the liquid around in the heavy crystal glass.

I stood in the doorway for a while. Taking in the details. Two ways in and out. Conventionally speaking, of course. In desperate times you could probably pull open those thick curtains and dive out the large French windows. Not that it would be my first choice. Diving through glass isn't like in the films. You get cut bad. You get *hurt*.

The television and stereo were tucked away in a corner that didn't dominate the room. Unusual in a modern home. The size of the screen was modest, too. I remembered Keller quoted in *The Dundee Herald* as talking about how multimedia ruined culture, so it figured he wouldn't give much prominence to flatscreen HD.

The sofa he was sitting on was a wine red. Looked like you could just sink into it after a hard day taking backhanders from crooked coppers and other assorted arseholes. Maybe he would have been relaxing on it now if he didn't have guests.

Then again, it was past three in the morning.

Burns said, "McNee, do come in. Peter's already got guests. The more the merrier."

Keller looked at me as best he could in his position. Trying to work out who I was. The same look I'd seen earlier that week from a junkie ex-cop. But Keller's eyes had more clarity than those of ex-cop and current junkie Raymond Grant. The question in them was the same

163

though: *Who is this man?*

Burns said, to me, "Why don't you tell our host why you're here?"

I remained standing. Said simply, "Ernie Bright."

Got an immediate reaction from Keller. As though someone had run a current through that wine-red sofa. He didn't loosen the grip on that blood-stained hankie, but he came close.

I said, "What happened to your nose anyway? You have an accident?"

Burns looked at me. A warning in his expression. Some people, when they want you to play along, they have this begging look about them. Burns didn't have such a look. If I didn't do as he wanted, I'd be as much in the shite as Keller. Maybe more.

Burns said, "These things happen. Later at night. Maybe after a couple of glasses. He'll be fine. Nothing important, eh?" This last question directed at Keller.

I said, "Give me five minutes."

Burns looked at me again. Eyebrows raised. Unguarded surprise.

I hoped that might appeal to his vanity, the idea that someone could still surprise him. Especially someone in whom he believed he saw something of himself. "Five minutes?"

I said, "I know what you want. I can get it from him."

Keller let loose a strangled whimper. Of course he was scared. He didn't know who I was. He'd heard my name, but clearly didn't recognise it. To him I was just another associate of David Burns. Another man who wanted information. Another thug who would be prepared to hurt Keller to get what I wanted.

All of which worked to my advantage.

When Keller looked at me, he saw the bruises, probably figured I looked this way all the time. If he asked what happened, he would imagine me coming out with some line like, "You should see the other guy."

164

Which was why he didn't ask the question. Didn't put on any false bravado.

He just made this pathetic little noise. A balloon with the final puff of air making its escape.

I said again to Burns, "Five minutes."

Burns said, "I could do with a cigarette," as he stood up.

The old man gave me the warning look again as he left the room. *Don't screw with me.* Aye, I had a certain amount of trust banked with the man but if I went over the score, he'd deal with me like anyone else. Burns was enough of a sociopath to turn off his empathy at will.

When we were alone and the door was shut, I sat down in the seat that Burns had vacated and leaned forward so that I was looking directly at Peter Keller.

The politician finally removed the hankie from his nose in a tender, careful movement. The flow of blood had slowed to a trickle. He sat very still, as though afraid any sudden movement might set it off again.

As though any sudden movement might set *me* off.

I said, "We have five minutes. So you're going to tell me about Ernie Bright and Kevin Wood. You're going to give me everything I ask for. That way, we both might make it to the morning alive."

TWENTY-FIVE

1973.

Peter Keller graduated from St Andrews University. PhD in political science and a plan to "change this country for the better." In his case, "for the better" meant actively campaigning for a Conservative government. Even decades after the Thatcher administration he'd be one of those who cried out the "more good than harm" line as everyone with half a brain remembered "Maggie Thatcher, milk snatcher" and other, worse slogans that came to epitomise the perceived idiocy and greed of the Tory administration. Keller got involved in local level politics after he moved to Dundee with his fiancée, the two of them sharing a small flat in the city's West End. She helped support the move by finding a job teaching English at a local secondary. They were a young couple on the up.

Keller became involved in the local council later that year. Campaigned long and hard in his ward, promising more than he could ever hope to deliver. But he found that it wasn't the voters who made his life better. Rather, it was those individuals for whom he could do small favours; nothing more than turning a blind eye here or making a subtle recommendation there. Okay, you needed a degree of amorality to do it, but Keller found that came naturally, especially when the price was right.

It was a good life.

Until the police came knocking on his door.

In 1975, Kevin Wood was a beat copper. A uniform, but with a future. Not because of his work – although everyone would say that he was a fine copper – but because he was kissing all the right arses, whispering all the right seductions in all the right ears.

But what no-one in the chain of command suspected was that he was also playing the streets. How else do you explain his showing up at the door armed with hard evidence of Keller's complicity in some of the shadier development deals of the last few years?

"When I opened the door to him," Keller said, "he was smiling. You'd think he was bloody Dixon of Dock Green popping in for tea and crumpets. What I remember was that he smiled. And it should have been warm and reassuring, but it made me want to turn and run. And not just because he was an ugly sod."

Wood had documents that proved beyond a doubt the facts of Keller's corruption: under-the-table deals, development opportunities he'd passed through against formal recommendations, motions he'd carried on behalf of others, records obtained for the wrong people. Minor league stuff, but enough to get Keller in trouble if it ever fell in front of the right people.

"People like me don't go to prison," Keller told me, over thirty years later, his voice shaking. His idea of prison probably came from popular rumours and tales of hell that circulate like a game of Chinese whispers until the thought of prison becomes, in its own way, worse than the reality. "We're not made for it. Not brought up for it. We can't survive."

I wanted to reach out and smack him. The presumed arrogance. The idea that "people like him" don't go to prison. Twenty-first century arseholes like Keller still cling desperately to Victorian ideas of class. For a supposedly classless and modern society, we still breed morons who presume privilege and right above others just because of the family and wealth they were born to.

I said, "So you went along with what he wanted because he had dirt on you?"

Keller said, "Yes."

All it took was the threat of violence to get a man like this to do whatever you want. I'd read the interviews in the papers, seen him sometimes on the TV, and he always spoke with such presumed authority about the moral backbone of society. When Cameron proposed "the big society" after his Conservative/Liberal coalition took power, Keller had been omnipresent across the local media saying that, finally, we had a Government who would "give responsibility back to the people." I'd not been convinced then. Liked what he stood for even less now.

Ernie used to tell me, "the only thing worse than a criminal of any kind is a hypocrite."

He was right. Looking at the prime example sitting across from me, I wanted to grab Keller, tell him how he was a fucking disgrace. His spineless fear and lack of anything approaching dignity had cost so many lives. And that one in particular mattered to me. Directly or not, he was responsible for the death of a man I had respected. And loved.

But I held in the anger. Squashed it. Sat there silently. Not moving a muscle. Because, unlike Keller, I had principles.

Of morality.

Of professionalism.

And even if this case was purely personal, something that wasn't going to wind up pleasing my bank manager or gaining me any kind of reference, I had to treat it like any other. Because hypocrisy would not be tolerated.

So I forced myself to sit back. I was going to let the facts deal with themselves. I was going to remain detached. Like the good, *professional* investigator I'd always claimed to be.

The truth takes care of itself. In the job, you just have to accept that and deal with whatever ugliness emerges in the fallout.

I said, "You were scared? Wood's threats got to you?"

"I thought about standing up to him," Keller said. "Before you think the worst of me. I did. Truly. The things he asked me to do, I realised most of them were fronts or covers for other activities. While I wasn't doing anything worse than showing unexpected favouritism or perhaps occasionally pushing for one sponsor over another, that kind of thing, I realised I was contributing to some terrible things. Worse than anything I'd done before."

I resisted the urge to make some kind of accusation. "But these things never affected people you knew personally."

He tried to hide it. But I saw the twitch. He had to have accused himself of all these things and worse over the years. Here, away from TV cameras and press junkets, he was a man who had made bad choices. Maybe he felt the relief of not having to hide what he'd done. I was giving him the chance to unload all his guilt on someone who wanted to listen.

A priest. Or a psychiatrist. Whichever, sometimes the investigator has to play both roles. Aye, pick your poison.

But his confession wouldn't be about absolution. He knew that. I couldn't forgive him. I don't know that there's anyone who could. But by unloading his guilty secrets, he might be able to find some peace when he was alone with nothing but his memories.

He said, "I did think about it. I had it all planned out what I was going to say. I was going to come home, call him and arrange a meeting. I had the location all planned out. I had a script. I'd spend most of my day locked in the office at HQ, ostensibly working on campaign funding but what I'd been doing was finding the words, the threats, I wanted to make. It would have been good, too." He smiled; an oddly gentle smile, like a person might find flickering across their faces when they remember a particularly stupid incident from their childhood. One that, at the time, had been mortifying, but now seemed like the gentle folly of youth.

Because in the end, he did nothing. His grand gesture to escape from the mire of corruption never materialised.

The way Keller told it, he'd been getting antsy for months about some of the things he was doing for his new friend. All the same, he admitted to me that he'd forced himself to remained wilfully ignorant of what was the obvious truth. "But who wouldn't? We were all in it, to one degree or another."

He dropped the name of another politician, this one a little older, who'd gone on to the national stage, become something of a personality in the world of politics. Told me about some of the man's dodgy deals, how nothing had ever really stuck to him. "The world of MPs' expenses," Keller said, and if he hadn't been so nervous, he might even have laughed, "is that storm in the teacup you keep hearing about. I mean, it's the equivalent of bloody Al Capone being taken down for tax evasion."

I nodded. Let Keller keep talking. About the day he finally tried to stand up to Kevin Wood.

He'd spent most of the day psyching himself for the deed. Had it all planned.

He would make the call from a box at the end of the road. Back then, it was not too hard to find a phone box. These days, the few in the city centre are rarely used and in the west end these days, there's one of the old red designs at the end of Forest Park Road that's become more a modern art installation than anything useful.

"I didn't even think about the car at the end of the road. Just ignored it. Back then we were on our way up, you know. Top floor flat at the end of a row of tenements that had become nicely middle class. Everyone had cars. It wasn't unusual." Except this one didn't belong to anyone on his street and it was only later he'd realise the make and model was well out of reach of any of his neighbours' annual incomes. "When I walked in, the wife called me through to the living room. I thought she just wanted to say hello. I walked in, found her sitting there drinking tea with Wood."

"Did she know about him?"

"Know what?"

"Who he really was. What he was all about."

Keller shook his head. "He was nothing more than a cop to her. A friend of mine. One of those contacts I'd made when I was out electioneering. She had no idea..." He looked at me, and there was this sudden pleading in his face. "She still doesn't."

I wondered where his wife was this evening. I figured she had to be out, couldn't be upstairs and asleep. She'd have been woken by now. But our time together was running out. I let Keller talk.

"He was there, grinning that grin that I guess she found reassuring. She said how nice it was of him to pop round, and he did this whole bloody act like, *aw I feel bad this isn't just a social call but I need to talk to Peter about work.*" Keller shook his head at the memory. "Christ, he was a slimy bugger when he wanted to be."

"What happened?"

"We talked in the back room. The one we'd converted into an office where I could do my work at night. Because there are no hours in politics, no real nine-to-fives. You have to understand that, right?"

"I know the feeling."

Keller's brow creased a little and he looked at me as though it was the first time he'd realised I was in the room. Starting to realise that he didn't know who or what I really was.

The minute a subject starts to think about their situation, to have any thought concerning anything other than the answer to your questions, an interview is in danger. It's when people are relaxed, when they're not thinking

171

about who they're talking to or where they are that they open up more. It doesn't matter whether they think you're a friend or they just don't care who's in the room, the minute they start to think, there's every chance they'll just quit jawing and do the stony silence gig on you.

But Keller's hesitation lasted only a moment. He *wanted* to talk. I don't think he cared any more. Figured he was a dead man whatever he did.

He said, "He closed the door. He'd been talking to me in front of the wife like we were old mates, and then he closes the door and he grabs me. He was stronger than he looked. Shoved me against the wall. His hands on my throat." As he spoke, Keller probed at his throat with the tips of his fingers as though he could still feel the bruises there. Decades later, I thought maybe he did.

Wood had told Keller that he knew what was going on. That he wasn't stupid. That Keller needed to get it into his head that there was nowhere he could turn. "If I go down, you're coming with me. D'you get that? Does that enter into your thick bloody head?"

All Keller could do was nod.

Keller, as I'd already figured, was not a strong man. Any ideas he'd had about playing the hero, about turning around an already messed up situation, vanished. He didn't take well to threats. He was afraid. Afraid of being hurt. Afraid of having to face up to the consequences of his actions.

Never discount fear as a motivation for criminal behaviour. Some villains can be like spiders in that way. More frightened of you than you are of them.

Keller spent the next couple of decades in Wood's pocket. Along the way, he learned more than he ever cared to. What he knew could bring down some of the most powerful men in the Dundee underworld.

"That's what your boss wants with me, yeah? I know things have been bad for a while, that him and Wood have had this kind of unofficial truce..."

"...But the situation's been building?"

Keller said, "You could say that, aye. Lately, Wood's been grabbing up new builds and developments, squeezing competition to make room for his own people. He's got his finger in a lot of pies."

"But there are layers between the man himself and his source of income."

"He's not an idiot."

"He's kept himself clean. You're one of the few people directly involved with illegal activity that I think he's had personal contact with."

"He said we had a special relationship." He almost choked on the words.

"But you never came forward?"

Keller hung his head. "Because if he went down, so would I." He licked his lips, as though suddenly dehydrated. "People like me don't do well in prison."

"You said that." I tried to keep my disgust in check. "So Wood's been making a grab for more power? That's why the conflict stepped up between him and..." I jerked my head to the door where Burns had left the room.

"Wood kept telling me he could take the old git down. Legally, I mean."

I shook my head. "David Burns is too good for that." Thinking that if Wood and Burns had ever agreed on anything, then they'd have been unstoppable.

Keller said, "That's why you're on his payroll? Forgive me, but you seem smarter than the average thug."

I knew what Keller had taken me for but to hear him say it out loud was a sucker punch that knocked me off my feet. I tried not to let it show, just said, "I need to ask you something."

"What, you wanted to know about me and Wood?"

"Think a man like Burns would come here for your life story?" I played it hard, talking up the tough act. Coming in close so that he backed off. "Someone was killed recently. Murdered. A police detective. Was getting close to Wood. To his... extra-legal activities."

That got him. Keller took in a deep breath, sharp enough that it could have sliced his insides. His eyes went wide. He said, "Bright."

"He was here?"

"Asking questions."

"What happened?"

"I answered them."

"And?"

Keller hung his head.

I just needed the spineless little shite to say what I already knew.

I waited.

Just long enough.

"I called Kevin Wood," Keller said, and he couldn't look me in the eye as he spoke. "I didn't know what –"

"Spare me," I said. No more time for pussy-footing around this prick. I let the disgust out. Not enough that I spat on him, but the thought did cross my mind. "Spare me, you prick. You hypocritical little fuck. You knew exactly what would happen."

"I didn't, I –"

"Fuck you!" I went to the door. It opened before I arrived. Burns walked in. Smiling.

"My turn," the old man said to me.

I stood there. "No," I said. "No fucking way."

Burns said, "Then what do we do with him?"

"I told you," I said. "This gets handled the way Ernie would have wanted."

Burns shook his head. "Chrissakes," he said. "You're a stubborn little bastard, McNee. What if I told you that deep down, your precious DCI Bright knew the truth; that street justice is the only real justice there is. He understood that, you know. Underneath his sanctimonious prick exterior. That's why we were friends, despite everything. Because he knew and understood same as I do. He just didn't want to accept it. Deliberately wore the blinkers,

174

maintained the illusion because he was scared of what it might mean to finally admit the truth." Burns took me by both shoulders, spun me so that we were facing each other. In his head, I think he thought it was a fatherly gesture.

Except this man wasn't my father. Not even close.

Burns said, "You're just the same, McNee."

I shrugged him off. Walked over to Keller. "This spineless eejit's coming down to FHQ. You can stay or you can come with. Either way, he's going down, and he's going to talk to someone about what he knows and we're going to take down Kevin Wood by the letter of the law. We're going to show him that the law means something."

Burns laughed. And then, as though talking to a son he couldn't help but indulge, he said, "If it takes the cunt out, then we'll do it your way. But I think Wood's smarter than you give him credit for. And in case you've forgotten, it was a brother in blue who tried to kill you earlier this evening. You tell me who you can trust."

I said, "I'll take the chance."

"You've either got balls of brass," Burns said, "or you're a suicidal bastard."

"Well?"

He studied me for a moment. "I'm still not sure."

"We move now," I said. "Wood's already in motion; he's got to realise something's up. Sooner or later, he'll figure that we've got to Keller."

"My lad'll do the driving," Burns said.

The muscle grabbed Keller roughly. I wanted to tell him that he didn't have to play it that way, that Keller was coming willingly. But given some of the admissions I'd heard this evening, I figured Keller might just deserve a little rough treatment.

Burns said, "I have some other business to take care of." He looked to his associate. "I can drive myself." Then, to me: "I think its something you need to be involved in."

"No," I said. "I need to be there when –"

"This isn't a double-cross or any other kind of shite,"

Burns said. "I'm a man of my word." He believed it, too. And in a way he was right. David Burns was a man of his word. When it suited him to be so.

I hesitated.

He said, "You want to see this through to the end? Be the hero?"

I didn't know where to go.

Burns said, "There's one more link, you know."

"Aye?"

"The trigger man."

"You know who he was?"

Burns raised his eyebrows. An intimate gesture that somehow became a challenge at the same time.

Did I have a choice?

We walked outside. All of us. The muscle leading Keller to the garage. Burns and I stood just outside the porch and watched in silence. Burns sparking up. He didn't offer me any this time. In the cool of the early morning air, I could have done with a little warmth

I heard the doors slam, a couple of seconds later the choke of an engine starting.

And then...

There was a jolt in the pit of my stomach, the kind you get when a rollercoaster topples over the edge of that long drop.

I don't remember anything like a punch or a sudden pressure pushing me forward. All I knew was the drop. The sensation of weightlessness. My ears popped so that for a moment all I could hear was a dull roar. It seemed to come from far away, maybe even across the other side of the city.

Then I hit the ground. The grass was damp between my fingers. The shockwave took a moment to vibrate from my arse up. Not painful so much as dull.

I watched the flames belch from the garage and the black smoke plume out in a kind of beautiful and terrifying choreographed movement. My eyes were drawn to the bright flame against the dark of the background, and the choking thickness of that smoke that seemed darker than anything else the evening had to offer.

I felt as though I'd been flung through water, plunging down and slowing as I went deeper, ready for the inevitable rise back to the surface.

When I broke it, the real world intruded with the intensity of a lightning bolt.

It started with the noise. I was suddenly all too aware of the crackling and burning from the garage, and the black smoke started to spread out, to chase me down, try and force its way in through my mouth and nose, soot and particles gagging up my nose and throat.

I felt the agony in my back from where I'd landed wrong, the pain in my wrist where I'd taken pressure from the fall.

I turned my head and saw David Burns next to me. He was laid out on his stomach, as though he'd had the presence of mind to turn away from the blast when it happened. Maybe he had, at that. David Burns was no stranger to sneak attacks.

In the mid-80s, he'd been sent letter bombs. Ostensibly the work of an IRA contact he'd burned bad on an arms deal. Of course, the culprit was never formally identified or caught and there never was any evidential connection between David Burns and any terrorist organisation, Irish or otherwise.

Burns pushed himself up, twisting so that he could look towards the explosion. He forced himself into a sitting position and just stayed there, his jaw dropped, his eyes wide with surprise and shock.

I watched him more than the fire.

As his expression hardened again. As he reasserted his authority, slipping back his mask and his bluster like a suit of armour that had momentarily come undone revealing something of the real man underneath. A man who was as afraid of death as anyone else. A man who did not expect such viciousness. Who could not conceive why anyone would want to attack him.

He turned to me. "So much for doing it your way."

I swallowed, looked back at the fire.

Already, I could hear sirens.

There was nothing else I could do.

I fell onto my back, looked up at the night sky. For a moment I believed the earth might just swallow me up, take me away from all of this. Let it all finally just end.

TWENTY-SIX

You don't walk away from a crime scene.

What you do is you stay where you are. Offer open arms and, more importantly, open mouth. You give the attending officers no reason to doubt your intentions.

On that last point, admittedly, I was screwed.

Not just given my history. Given my company.

They separated us. Burns had stuck around, despite my worries that he'd try and make a run for it, pretend like he was never there. Maybe the explosion shocked him more than he was prepared to admit. Or maybe he was playing the game the best way he knew: acting like the innocent he wanted everyone to believe he was.

Whatever the case, we weren't given a chance to talk once the coppers showed up. *Divide and conquer* remains the cornerstone of interrogating multiple witnesses.

Or suspects.

I was sitting in the back of a Panda when the front door opened and a DI climbed in the passenger seat. He turned and grinned at me.

I said, with no inflection, "Molly."

He twitched. The side of his face spasmed involuntarily. He said, "That's DI Mollison to you." Didn't matter that he had a head like a slab of concrete and shoulders to could support it, he was stuck with the name "Molly". I don't even know if it was his real name, but the rumour his parents had a strange sense of humour, figured there was some truth to that Johnny Cash song about a boy named Sue and gave their lad the kind of name he'd have to fight to get respect for.

"You want to tell me," Molly said, "what you were doing here?"

"Privileged information," I said. "Confidential. Between me and my client."

"And your client is that crooked old sod talking to DS Soutar in the back of the van?"

I shrugged.

Giving nothing away. Knowing that whatever I did, Molly Mollison was going to try and twist it.

"Hey, McNee," Molly said, "I know your reputation. Pain in the arse. The last sheriff in town. Whatever, but maybe it's time you started talking. Because whenever you're involved in something, it tends to go to hell. Let's make this the one time that things end well, that the real bad guys go to prison and no-one ends up paying for your mistakes."

That last one a clumsy jab.

Susan had told me how a few years ago she and Molly had gone out on a couple of disastrous dates. Disastrous, at least, from her point of view. Molly'd always seemed pretty keen for another try, and in the end she found she had to sit him down and explain that she couldn't return his feelings.

I said, "You sure you're not making this personal?"

"I haven't even started."

I gave Molly the edited highlights of my evening.

He listened without interruption. The worst kind of interview is someone who's wise to your tricks, who knows the game. A career criminal. Or an ex-cop.

So he played it simple. And just let me talk.

"What I don't understand," he said when I finished, "is what you were doing here in the first place."

Like I said, I didn't give Molly the whole truth. In part because something Burns had said was itching at the back of my skull. A consistent irritation that grew worse the less attention I tried to give it.

...in case you've forgotten, it was a brother in blue who tried to kill you earlier this evening. You tell me who you can trust.

Molly had never struck me as corrupt. But there's truth in all those old clichés about appearances being deceptive.

"I told you, it's confidential between —"

"You and your client. Right."

Outside, the fire service tamed the blazing garage. Ambulances were on standby with the desperate illusion of hope. Neighbours had gathered at the edges of the tape, watching with folded arms, theirs eyes wide with expectation.

Everyone present knew the truth. Keller was already dead. You didn't have to be a forensic expert to figure the incident was far from accidental. And you definitely didn't need to be Columbo to know that the only witnesses were holding back vital information.

It's hard to bluff when everyone already knows your cards.

Molly, in the front seat, turned away from me and looked out the front windshield. He said, "I'd have thought you'd be with Susan this evening. Given everything that's happened."

Molly was divorced. It would have been a cheap shot to bring up his suitability to offer any kind of relationship counselling, but I could feel it on the edge of my voice, wanting to creep up and lash out at this bastard.

I held it in. Gave him nothing.

Said, "What do you think about what happened to Ernie?"

Molly grunted.

I pressed: "You have to have an opinion. The old bugger was found in possession of narcotics and a shiteload of money. Had a hole blown in his chest. Was found at a location best described as remote. Hadn't told anyone where he was going. He wasn't working drugs. His undercover days were so far behind him he probably couldn't remember them. You tell me what you think happened, Mollison." Using his last name. It wasn't a dig. It was a direct request.

Because I wanted to know. Wanted to hear him say it.

He said, "I want it to be a misunderstanding."

I said, "But?"

"But it's like that old Chuck Berry number. You never can tell." Molly turned back to me. "Sometimes you can think you know someone, McNee, and then they turn around and do something so stupid you have to wonder if you ever really knew them at all."

Was he talking about Ernie?

I'd never really worked with Mollison. Our paths had occasionally crossed at morning briefings and on a few social occasions. He had a reputation as a guy with a temper, and most of the younger coppers had kept their heads down in his presence.

I'd watched him in interviews, seen the way he adapted his technique. He came off as little more than a brick shit-house; and then you could see him reach out and connect with some guy, fake empathy to the degree that even if you knew it was a trick, you started to wonder.

I said, "Could you understand it, though? If he was tempted?"

Molly didn't turn to face me. "Don't you bloody well start," he said. "I know you think you're better than us, now. A few articles in the paper calling you a hero; you start believing your own press. Aye, and then you start to think about things you saw, and half-whispered intimations you overheard. There's always going to be corruption in the force, McNee. Don't think I'm an eejit. I know what happens. The temptations that can come with the job, the power it brings. But I also know that Ernie Bright was a good man. I thought that you'd at least have enough respect to remember it, too."

I had no response.

After a few moments, he said, "I could hold you without charge."

"But you're not going to."

He shook his head. "I take you in," he said, "And it's because I have something to charge you with other than being a pillock in the wrong place at the wrong time."

I said, "Thank you."

"Don't you dare," he said, his voice low, his tone trembling as his anger fought to break loose. "Don't think of that as a chance or a sign that I respect you beneath the fucking bluster. Don't take it for any of that." He twisted round again. "Because I know you've been lying to me. Not all of it, of course. But enough to hide the lies."

I nodded. He got out, came round and opened the door.

As I climbed out, I asked, "How's DI Lindsay?"

"Aye, now you ask, eh?" He hesitated, as though uncertain whether he should tell me. "Touch and go."

"I'm sorry," I said.

"Sod it," Molly said, standing aside to let me past.

I found it hard to walk in a straight line. From the moment I stood up, without support, I found that the world had started spinning faster than I expected. It was like being drunk with the bright glow of supreme confidence or the gentle glow of a strong drink nestling in my stomach.

Instead all I had was a dead weight in my stomach and a feeling like my legs couldn't support the weight, that they were going to collapse beneath me and I was never going to be able to get back up.

But I did it, walked away from the car and the clean-up crew and back onto the street. I got into my own car and once the door was closed, I took some deep breaths. Felt my eyelids getting heavy, but knew I couldn't close them.

If I did, there would be the temptation to keep them closed.

TWENTY-SEVEN

Back at the flat, the lights were off. Susan wasn't waiting up.

I checked my watch.

Six in the morning. Daylight would be coming soon. There was a hint of it in the horizon, colour licking into the dark blue of the night sky.

How long without sleep, now? All I wanted to do was crash. Stay in bed for the next week.

I didn't bother turning on the lights as I entered. I walked through the flat slowly, relying on the low illumination that came through from the living room where the open curtains let in the streetlights from outside.

In the bedroom, my eyes adjusted enough that I could distinguish the shape of the bed. I pulled back the covers.

Hesitated.

I'd thought Susan was asleep. But she wasn't in the bed. The covers were rumpled because neither of us had bothered to make the bed from earlier. There was no trace of heat. The sheets were cold.

But I figured she'd be back. And all I wanted to do was sleep. So I crawled into the bed, pulled the covers tight over me. Shivering just a little.

After a while, my own body heat stopped the shivering. Underneath the blankets I felt safe. Secure.

My eyelids were heavy. I couldn't have opened them if I wanted to.

I thought maybe I should call Susan.

But it was too late.

Sleep came.

#

I thought only seconds had passed. But it was dark when I opened my eyes, and I realised I had slept through the day.

Susan was not beside me. The bedside clock displayed the time in angry red numerals.

My stomach rumbled.

I moved into the kitchen. Grabbed a ready-meal curry from the fridge and shoved it in the microwave. Normally I'd think about cooking for myself. But as long as I'd slept, I didn't feel rested, and my body was still shaking like something had gone wrong inside me.

When the curry was ready, I spooned it onto a plate and went through to the living room. The flat felt empty. I knew instinctively that Susan had not been here since my return.

That was when I saw the note on the fold-away table near the window. I put down my plate and unfolded the paper. Susan's handwriting was neat, with the kind of attention to detail I could strive for and never attain. She told me it was something that had just come naturally to her.

I unfolded the note, smoothed it out on the table. Stayed standing as I read:

Steed,

If anyone can understand, I think it's you. My father is dead. Unlike you, I know who is responsible.

Thank you for all you have done. But I can't just sit here and mourn. If my dad taught me anything it was that you

185

have to do what you know is right.

She didn't sign off with "love", or any other words that would have rung falsely, ended the letter on a note of uncertainty. Just her name.

It was enough, I think.

Enough for me to understand.

#

"Tell me what you'd do, if you ever found the driver of that vehicle?"

The doctor had his legs stretched out, crossed at the ankles. He was sitting back in that chair, arms behind his head. All casual. Unintentionally smug.

It was a few months after the accident. The counselling was mandatory. I was a few sessions away from quitting, the carefully portioned, methodically directed hours all blending into one long conversation that seemed to ramble all over the shop, with no clear direction that I could ever make out. Just when I thought I had a handle on where this guy wanted me to go, he'd weave onto another topic without giving me time to adjust.

Of course, you have to figure that maybe that was the point.

I tried to think about the answer.

Going against everything this guy wanted. He was after the gut reaction, working on the principle that the unguarded mind gives away its deepest secrets.

He wanted me to open up.

I heard somewhere that Freud claimed the Irish were the one people for whom psychoanalysis was of no use whatsoever. I figured he hadn't met a Scotsman.

We despise the idea of opening up. Of people knowing us. Getting the very heart of whatever it is that makes us tick. Try and get close to a Scotsman, he'll probably wind up further away from you than he was before.

The doc said, "There's no judgement in here. You can't

186

be rebuked for your thoughts."

I took a breath. "You want the truth? I'd want some time alone with him."

"Oh?"

I was tensed up. The room was too small, not enough air for two men to breathe. Why didn't he open a bastarding window?

He used my first name. The word became an interrogatory. I hadn't let anyone call me by that name in a long time. Made me sit up and pay attention. I said. "I mean I'd beat the shite out of him. I mean I'd slam my fists into his face until he understood only half of what I feel."

The doc nodded. Utterly calm. Only made me feel worse. He said that there was no judgement. But that wasn't true. What he meant was that there would be no judgement aired. But we always judge other people. Even if we say nothing, no-one remains neutral about another human being.

The silence was overwhelming.

It was an old trick, one we used in interrogation, and I knew all he was doing was waiting me out because in the end I'd have to fill the silence with something. But I couldn't last.

I was fucked up. He knew it. And whether I admitted it or not, I knew it too.

It was one of the reasons I suddenly backtracked and justified myself even though I didn't need to. "I know it's wrong. I know it goes against everything I've ever believed, but all I want to do is find that bastard, break his face, put my hands around his throat and throttle the life out of him."

"And what do you think that will achieve?"

I hesitated. For real this time. Not searching for what I thought might be an expected answer, but suddenly genuinely unsure.

Stuck for an answer.

Susan had been there for me after Elaine's death. Yes, we drifted apart after one mistake neither of could face up to at the time. But she had seen another human being in pain and she had tried to do something for them. It wasn't merely about offering sympathy, but about being there. Soaking up some of that grief. Because she cared.

And now?

She had suffered. Loss. Betrayal. Grief.

And where had I been? What had I done for her?

I had taken her grief and twisted it into my own. Selfish bastard I was. Acting as though her loss was mine.

I should have been there for her.

Why hadn't I realised? Too wrapped up in myself? Same old story. Made me sick just thinking about it: realising what I was. The selfishness and hypocrisy disgusted me as much as Peter Keller had done.

Susan had been left alone with her grief. Allowed it to simmer. She had no outlet. No release. No-one to help her.

I had let her down.

Grief is a strange state. A momentary insanity. Your actions become unpredictable. While there are five recognised stages, they don't all act out the same way. Grief is far from mechanical. It is chaotic. It is insanity.

I read Susan's note over and over.

The words burned into my eyes. I could have recited them word for word without ever looking at them again.

Because I understood everything that she wasn't saying. All the words she didn't dare write.

I had tasted revenge. It was something I had sought for a long time. It had finally been ersatz, exacted on a substitute for the real source of my anger, leaving me empty and unfulfilled. More ill-at-ease with the world. Somehow removed because of the things I had done.

For a long time after, I had dreamt of Elaine. She would stand over me while I slept, her expression... not angry. Just... sad. I wanted to wake up and tell her that

I had done it for her. But I always knew that she didn't want to hear that.

The dream had faded with time. But the empty sensation had not.

The only person to pull me back had been Susan. In spite of everything, she made me feel a little less disconnected to the world. She had become my anchor. Even before we began sleeping together, she had been there for me. A reminder of what I wanted the world to be. Of the best that people could be.

Susan had been everything that I was not. I should have learned from her.

Maybe it wasn't too late.

TWENTY-EIGHT

I blinked, brought the world outside back into focus. Despite spending the daylight hours beneath the bedsheets, all I wanted to do was sleep. Curl up in a corner and close my eyes.

My body was trying to tell me to just give up. Finally admit defeat.

But I couldn't do that. After reading the note, I knew there was no time. What I had to do was consider the next move.

And not give in to panic.

There was no reply from Susan's mobile.

"This is Susan Bright. I can't answer right now. Leave a message."

I dialled three times, before finally giving up. Trying to think of a new plan.

The message echoed about my head, as though part of me thought it was important, that there was some clue in her words that was escaping me.

My head was light, ready to float off my shoulders. My muscles trembled like the temperature had dropped dramatically. But it wasn't cold. It was adrenaline rush. And I couldn't ignore it. I had to do something.

What I did was leave the flat, head to the street, to my car.

Only when I was in the driver's seat, I hesitated.

Thinking: *Where would she go?*

Under normal circumstances, she might have gone to see someone she trusted. Try and get a new perspective on her feelings.

Maybe someone like Lindsay. She used to tell me how he was a good sounding board. That there was no bullshit in his advice.

I'd always scoffed at that.

But Lindsay was in the hospital, in a coma, under constant surveillance. From both sides of the law, if I was to believe everything that Burns had told me.

He had nothing to give her. No support. No wisdom. Not even a formal dressing down for thinking like an eejit.

I couldn't think of anyone else. Except her father.

While she and her mother were close, I knew they never really confided in each other. Susan had always been her daddy's girl.

So where was she?

It was obvious, I suppose, but I kept dancing around the answer. Frightened by what it might mean.

But it was not the time to be scared. Not if I wanted to make up for not having been there earlier. Knowing that if I had been, I could have stopped this going so far.

I started the car's engine. The wipers brushed away raindrops into blurred streaks on the windscreen.

The streets were quiet this late at night, save for taxis and a few folks who'd been working late or were maybe even just heading out. At Dot's insistence, I'd recently outfitted the car with GPS. Program in your destination, the computer tells you where to go. Not always the best route, and I knew from listening to the news that these systems were notorious for driving people into lakes and across private property, but like anything else you just had to keep your wits about you and you'd be fine.

Which I guess was a problem for me, the way I felt.

But I kept myself focussed. Knowing where I wanted to go. Where this had been leading from the start.

"What would you do?"

"Hmmm?"

One year before the accident. Me and Ernie working paperwork on an investigation, drowning in background and irrelevant information, coming up for air because if we didn't we might never get to what we needed.

Sometimes the best way to get results is to walk away. If only for five minutes. Put the problem behind you.

Sometimes, it really seemed as though it solved itself.

"What would you do if they left you alone with the worst bawbag you could think of? No questions asked. No consequences."

I wouldn't recognise the same question rephrased two years later by a man I had been determined not to respect from the moment I walked into his office.

And even coming from a man whom I really did respect, I found it hard to get at the honest answer without feeling some pressure. As though there really was a right and a wrong way to respond.

"I don't know."

Ernie smiled at that. Benevolent. Giving nothing away, really. He said, "I've thought about that one a lot. About what I'd do."

"And?"

He said, "I don't know." He ran a hand through his hair, stretched and yawned, the back of his chair tipping as he did so. "I guess it depends on the bawbag, right?"

"You ever asked your daughter?"

"What she would do?" He sat forward again. Spun his chair so he was facing me. "The truth, McNee? I don't think I want to know. I hope I never do."

I've thought about his response a lot over the years. Susan was always a straight arrow, her sense of justice absolute and unswerving. But there were moments when I thought I saw another side to her. When she stood up to cover for Mary Furst and ultimately for me, it wasn't something I had expected. As though, for just a moment, she had become someone else entirely.

In interviews, I'd seen hard men give up close buddies, betray confidences, because of the way she looked at them. And sure, I told myself that it was an act and a bloody good one at that, but in quieter moments, I have to wonder if maybe they weren't somehow more perceptive than I gave them credit for. If maybe they hadn't glimpsed a side to Susan she hid from her colleagues, her friends, her loved ones.

Maybe Ernie had an idea of what his daughter was capable of.

Or maybe he was just tired after going through the facts of a gruelling case, didn't want to think about anyone he loved making the wrong decision. Because he knew what his own answer would be, despite his denial. And I think that scared him as much as anything else in the world.

#

There were lights on downstairs.

Wood lived maybe five miles out of the city. Aye, it cost bucks for a house like this, but he was gunning for Tayside's top cop job according to the rumours, and he had the cash to flash that went along with that responsibility.

I parked in the drive. Saw movement at the windows. A kitchen, by the look of it. The person moving was female. Late fifties, dark hair, wearing a heavy towelling dressing gown pulled tight against the cool of the encroaching evening.

As I stepped out of the car, the woman moved out of the kitchen and came to the front door. As she stepped into the night, I noticed she walked without fear or hesitation. A stranger turning up at this hour was not something she considered unusual.

I wondered what she knew about her husband. If she really understood his work.

"I don't know you," she said.

"Mrs Wood? I'm looking for your husband."

"Missed him."

"How long?"

"He got a call. It happens. You know, being a copper."

I said, "I know."

"You're on the job, then?"

"I was."

"He know you?"

I said, "You don't know where he went?"

"No."

"Has anyone else been here tonight?"

She had her arms folded across her chest. Suddenly on the defensive. Realising that maybe I wasn't who she first thought I was.

"Why?"

"I need to find your husband. Does he have a number I can –?"

"Who are you?"

I closed the car door and stepped forward. Keeping my body language open and neutral. I wanted her to see I wasn't here to hurt her husband.

Or her.

"Mrs Wood, how much do you know about what your husband does?"

#

She made me sit at the breakfast bar with my hands on the worktop, palms down. She kept her distance at all times, standing across the other side of the kitchen. I noticed how the knife block was in reach and the door was in dashing distance.

She was halfway to believing me, but it wasn't quite taking. Because I was a stranger Asking awkward questions to which she wished she didn't know the answers.

The house was warm, even if she couldn't feel it. The

heat came from the Aga that dominated their enormous, spotless kitchen.

"Tell me your name again."

I told her.

She looked at my card with half an eye, as though I'd be ready to take advantage of any lapse in concentration.

"And you're an investigator?"

"A private investigator. Used to be in the police. Like your husband."

"But you left?"

"It was a personal matter."

"And you think my husband's in danger?"

"I think he's been in danger for a very long time," I said. "But I think tonight there's someone out there who's about to do something they're going to regret."

"My husband can take care of himself."

"He's been doing that for decades," I said. "But he's not expecting this. Please, I just need..."

She took in a breath and held it. When she breathed out again, her shoulders relaxed a little. She said, "I'll call him. If this is a wind-up, though..."

"It's not," I said." I let my hands slip off the worktop. She didn't care or didn't notice. Either way it was encouraging.

She moved to the phone that was hanging on the wall near the door. Her eyes moved away from for a moment.

I stayed still. Let her make the call.

She turned to face me again after she'd dialled the numbers. Her face was calm at first, and then slowly I could see the wrinkles of worry appear in her forehead. They were deep, practised lines that formed after decades of concern.

She said, "He's not –" and then cut herself off. Spoke into the receiver, "Kevin, love, its Betty. Listen, you need to call me back. There's someone here and –"

I stood up.

She ended the call mid-sentence.

I didn't have the heart to tell her that he wouldn't be

calling back. Instead, I walked out of the house.

Into the dark.

#

She finally answered. My insistence paying off.

"Steed, you need to let me –"

"Where are you?"

"You don't need to be involved in any –"

"You know this is wrong."

"No," she said. "It's right. It's the bloody right thing to do."

"You've told me before to let the professionals handle these kinds of cases. You've told me that you can't become too close or –"

"Save it," she said. And I could hear a catch in her voice.

A noise rattled down the line. The sound of rattling steel and engines. Close to the phone, enough that it drowned out her voice. The noise came in low at first and then became loud enough that I winced. If I hadn't been on the hands free, I would have pulled the phone away from my ear. The noise filled up the inside of my car. But then it passed, and I got the impression that it had disappeared into the distance from wherever Susan was.

For a moment there was silence. Susan cleared the line. No goodbye. Just a click. And a dead line.

She knew I'd figured it out. At least, I had an idea where she was and what she was doing.

Maybe I could get to her in time. I had to believe that. Because, for once, things had to work out for the best. Like in the books, the movies, I needed justice and fairness and happiness.

Just once.

Just to remind me that life was worth it. That we weren't all fucked.

TWENTY-NINE

As the rail lines pass out of Dundee, heading west to the bridge, they elevate over the Kingsway and strike out across the water. There's a beautiful house built directly underneath the tracks as they rise above the dual carriageway that runs parallel to the riverside. At one time, I believe it used to be a guard's house. Whatever it once was, the house has always fascinated me. I'm rather taken with the idea that someone could live there with trains rumbling constantly overhead.

But I wasn't there that night to simply admire the local architecture.

Just past the house, as the tracks reach the zenith of their elevation, there. The spaces underneath the struts have been converted into a storage facility.

Following their split, Ernie's dad hired one of the lockups to keep some of the possessions he and Katie had collected down the years. Some were to be sold off. Others were to be divided up when cooler minds prevailed.

No-one hangs around the struts without business. Or, depending on their age, they're there to waste time and get high in a place where no-one's looking. Check the graffiti, you'd know this isn't somewhere you want to go at night.

Unless you have a very specific kind of business.

The gates to the yard were open. The chain busted.

Maybe a previous incident left unfixed, I couldn't be sure. I left the car parked outside the gates and pushed them all the way open. They scraped tight on the concrete..

Illumination came from the lights off the tracks that ran overhead. Assisted by the heavy black torch I had brought with me. I stepped inside the yard, my footsteps light and cautious.

Nothing moved.

I saw no sign of Susan's car. No sign of anything at all. "Hello? Susan?"

I kept still. Holding my breath. Listening close. Turned towards the sound of something banging; a rough sound with no real rhythm unless you could counted the syncopation of desperation. I walked towards the lockup where the sound was coming from.

"Hello?" I knocked on the door.

The banging increased. Frantic, now. Not against the door itself. No, the sound was muffled, as though whoever was making the noise was slamming against something inside the lockup, maybe the body of a car or a metal locker.

I checked the door number. Not that I needed to, of course.

Ernie's lockup.

I pulled at the door, twisted the handle. It rolled right up. The banging ceased.

Inside, I couldn't see anything. I blinked to let my eyes adjust. Flicked the torch around the interior.

The light ran over a figure hunched on the ground, next to a set of metal shelves against the east wall of the lockup. He'd been gagged, had been making a racket by slamming his weight against those shelves. Small objects had been knocked off these and onto the floor. Broken china and shards of glass glittered in the light of my torch.

I stepped forward for a better look at the man who had been left here, bound and gagged.

Kevin Wood was rail-thin, his now-grey hair cropped

short. Age hadn't been kind to him, but then youth hadn't been his finest hour, either; he'd always been an ugly bastard. He was covered in dust from the floor of the lockup. His face showed signs of what he'd been through. Swollen lips, open cuts, black eyes. His nose was misshapen and was gently trickling blood. Earlier, it had probably been a gush.

I reached down and pulled off his gag.

First words out of his mouth: "Fucking bitch cunt."

I reacted on instinct. Pulled my fist back. And then lashed out. The prick's head snapped back, and the shelves rattled as his weight crashed against them once more. For a moment I thought they might come loose and topple over, crushing the ugly bastard.

But they stayed standing.

More's the pity.

He sat up again, slowly. And spat. Something solid landed on the ground. A tooth perhaps. "You know her, then?"

"You know who she is?"

"That arsehole's daughter," he said. "Fucksakes, should have just done the whole family."

"You know who I am?"

"Think I'd be saying anything if I didn't, McNee? Christ, but you're a tenacious fucker, I'll give you that." He sounded a world away from the cool, controlled copper who loved to appear in the media and talk about how dedicated he was to public service. Sure, he came across as smarmy, but his act had been good.

Fooled everyone. Except, of course, those in the know.

Like Burns.

Like Ernie.

But no-one can wear a mask all the time. The inevitable truth: it always drops. Sometimes only for a moment. Sometimes, you can never replace it.

But in the end, a mask can only cover your true face for so long.

The Kevin Wood beneath the mask was like a wild animal, snarling and lashing out. The chains seemed somehow appropriate.

I said, "Why'd she leave you here?"

"She had other business."

"Such as?"

He was still for a moment. The fight went out of him. He didn't look at me. "She let me live in exchange for the trigger man."

The trigger man.

The man who killed her father.

I'd thought maybe all she wanted was a pop at Wood. But she was aiming deeper than that. More personal. She didn't give a toss for the corruption angle, or the decades of abuse of power. All she wanted was to get back at the man who had her father's blood on his hands.

Over the last few days I'd almost forgotten about the trigger man, obsessing over the conspiracy and the corruption. I'd wanted so desperately to connect Ernie's death to Burns.

Perhaps it burned differently after all these years, but I hadn't recognised that same old desire for vengeance trying to disguise itself as something higher and nobler. As though it had muted inside me, becoming a quiet and insistent whisper rather than a roaring, all-consuming cry for closure.

But even if I hadn't seen it in myself, I should have seen it in Susan.

"Give me his name."

Wood shook his head.

I insisted: "The name."

"Get to fuck."

I grabbed him by the collar, hauled him up so our faces were inches apart. My body protested at the movement. My left hand didn't want to close, so most of the heavy work was done with the right. I tried not to let the pain show.

"The name."

"Or what?"

"You know you're sodded anyway? That if the police don't come for you, David Burns will."

"Aye, because you're so close to the foosty old cunt."

"Piss off!"

But Wood was on a roll, maybe thinking he was like a shark with the scent of blood in the water: "I know he's been making overtures, that for whatever reason he thinks you'd be a fine addition to his network. But you won't go for it. If you had your way, you'd see him behind bars." He hesitated a moment. "Or dead."

I let Wood drop.

He landed with no dignity, but all the same he laughed. He wasn't about to give up his confidence, even if he knew I'd never believe it.

I had a number I never thought I'd use. But time was running out. This wasn't about revenge any more for me. Or that desire to lash out at the world.

Here and now it was about stopping someone making a bad mistake.

I keyed in the number. Let it ring.

"Aye?"

"I've got someone here who wants to talk." I put the phone on speaker, held it out to Wood. "Say hello."

"Who the fuck's —"

The voice on the other end of the line let loose a chuckle. Low at first, and then rising until it sounded like he wouldn't be able to stop.

Wood's eyes widened. "Cocksucker! Fucking bawbag bastards! Cunting arsewipes, I'm going to —"

"You're going to what, Kevin?" said the voice on the other end. "What do you think you're going to do? I knew my man here couldn't resist giving you what you deserve." Then, directed to me: "Where is he?"

I didn't say anything. Just looked at Wood. Offering a silent challenge. He stared back. I expected him to try and call my bluff. And maybe he was going to, but I think he caught something in my expression that made him hesitate.

When my hand made to pull the phone back towards me, he said, "I'll give you the name."

I closed the line. Hunkered down before him. Said, "This way, it's just the law you have to deal with."

He laughed at that. A short, bitter bark.

"The name. Or this time I tell him right out. And I walk away."

Wood's face contorted. He wanted to kill me. If his hands weren't bound, he might have done so. Instead, his features twisted and he spat out the name: "Mick the Mick," he said. "Irish prick. Did some time inside for sexual assault, came out a killer for hire."

"He works exclusively for you?"

"Aye, he'd say so. Probably does gigs on the side, know what these criminal types are like. Never trust them." Maybe it was supposed to be a joke. Neither of us was laughing.

"You have an address for him?"

"A number."

I shook my head. "You gave her an address."

"Why do you want to stop her?"

"Because she'll be making a mistake."

"Aye? Don't think I don't know you, McNee. That incident at the Necropolis, for example. One man dead, another badly injured? Sure, maybe the survivor wouldn't talk, but anyone with half a brain could figure what happened. Lindsay let you off. You know that, right? He fudged the report, the whole investigation. Just vague enough that he didn't need to press charges. The stupid prick seems to have a soft spot for you. What, you think you got off because you were innocent? Christ, the Chief Superintendent was screaming for your blood."

I could have laughed it off. Knowing that he was baiting me. I didn't doubt some of what he said was true, but

Lindsay wouldn't have been trying to protect me.

I said, "Just give me the address."

He shook his head. "Fuck you, then," and reeled off a street and house number.

I stood up.

"At least leave me the bloody torch!"

I tried not to smile as I rolled the door shut, and left the arrogant bastard there in the dark. Alone.

THIRTY

She hadn't killed Wood.

That was a good sign.

But then, it was hard to think of Susan as a killer. Like any copper, she had her own store of anger. This, in itself, was not a bad thing. Because you need anger to do the job. A healthy sense of antagonism is practically a requirement for effective policing. But it needs to be tempered. The edges have to be shaven off. Otherwise you become a thug in uniform; a disgrace to the job. You become like the late Cal Anderson.

I wondered what would happen to the bastard's body. One thing was certain: Burns would ensure it would never be found. There were many people connected to the old man who had disappeared without a trace over the decades. Sure, the modern cop shows would have you believe that sooner or later all your old skeletons come back to haunt you, but in Burns's case there could be dozens of bodies he would take with him when he finally died.

There were two others out there as well.

I would have believed one of them to be the trigger man. But then maybe Wood had some sense of propriety after all. Knew that it would take more than corruption for one cop to kill another. When the corrupt shitebag was finally charged, there would be deep feelings among the rank and file: an age-old conflict:

We don't send down our own.

The uniform is thicker than blood.

It's the same psychology as in families who don't want to turn on their own no matter what they've done. Except coppers are honour-bound to do something about their bad apples, no matter how they feel about it.

Kevin Wood would be safer in the hands of cops than anywhere else. They'd agonise over what to do with him, but in the end they wouldn't – they couldn't – hurt him. Both because he was one of their own and because anything they did to him would be scrutinised by a public enquiry.

Handing Wood over to the coppers was a lose-lose for them.

For him it was the best outcome to the worst day of his life.

He'd be wondering, of course, as he waited in the dark, whether I'd hand him to the police or Burns. Or whether I'd want to deal with him myself. He said he knew who I was, what I had done. But depending on who told him the stories, he might believe I was in some way dangerous.

And maybe I was.

I wondered what Susan had told him. If she'd told him anything. Or just left him there, wondering if he'd die alone amongst one man's long lost memories. She'd shown mercy of a sort.

But would she be able to exercise the same self-control with Mick the Mick? The man who shot her father?

#

Most people, when they come out of prison, seek out family or friends. Looking to get themselves back into the world; trade off old favours or loyalties and set themselves up once more.

But there's very few of them wind up in plush converted apartments on the top floor of old Victorian mansions. Of course, if Wood was to be believed, Mick the Mick came out of prison with a saleable skill, even if it wasn't one of those approved by the parole board.

And there was always someone willing to pay good money for a practiced killer.

I'd learn more about Mick in the months and years to come, as the chaos calmed and the truth floated gently to the calmed surface. What I'd learn was that he went inside a waster, a university dropout originally from County Cork who had turned to drug dealing almost by accident. At first, it had been to raise funds for his course. Later, he dealt narcoticcs because he dug the lifestyle. He abandoned his studies, set himself up as an independent trader. He did well enough, relying mostly on his gift of the blarney to keep him out of trouble.

But he was the kind of moron who was always destined to wind up in the nick. He had no control. And clearly he'd never seen *Scarface* or heard the hoary old maxim: *don't get high on your own supply*. In the end, Mick was arrested for sexual assault on a young woman. His defence that he'd been under the influence at the time and not in control of his own actions didn't wash with the court. Mick was sentenced to a year inside. The sentence was light, given that it was Mick's first recorded offence.

Bad decision.

Mick found it tough adjusting to life inside.

Prison life is not as notorious as its reputation suggests. Not for everyone. But there are elements of truth to the popular mythology. Put any people of a similar type together and you'll get forms of tribalism and struggles for power and domination. Men like Mick, who've never known that world, become easy targets for certain types of people.

Prison is supposed to change a man. That's the whole idea. So from a certain point of view, then, you could count

Mick as a success story. His sentence wasn't long, wasn't supposed to be arduous, but after three months inside, Mick found himself with his back to the wall being threatened by a particularly violent prisoner. With his life on the line, Mick dug deep and found his dark side again. Broke the other man's neck in what the prison officials described as "a particularly brutal assault".

Funny how brutal a man can turn when he thinks he has nothing left to lose.

Mick's sentence was increased accordingly after the incident.

So, aye, prison changed him. He learned control. He learned direction. He learned violence. He learned patience.

Mick came out clean as a whistle. No more drugs for Mick. A changed man. No longer a drug addict.

Instead, he'd become a killer.

And he owed Kevin Wood, too. During his time inside, as his rep grew, he'd done a few jobs for Wood. Nothing too big. But he was rewarded handsomely. Assured of employment on the outside.

His first job being to get rid of a copper who'd been sniffing around places he had no right being.

It had been Wood's idea to plant the drugs near the murder scene.

After all, it's not enough to kill a man. No, Wood knew that to really hurt a man like Ernie Bright, you had to destroy him completely.

#

"You're with the police?"

I shook my head as I clambered out of the car.

I had to grip at the bodywork to keep upright. My legs were shaking. The skin across my forehead was stretched tight. My skull ached. How the hell was I still standing?

The man had run from across the road, his head ducked

as though afraid of the sky falling on him. He was pale, the kind of pale that comes from being awake early in the morning. He was wearing backless slippers and pyjamas beneath a thick dressing gown. I noticed the ends of the gown's sleeves were ratty, as though he picked at them. Judging from his quick, jerky movements, this man was a born worrier, the kind of guy who thought everything through. Probably spent so long thinking about things he missed a lot of opportunities for action.

He stayed down, hiding behind my car. I couldn't quite figure what he was doing. I turned to look at the old house that had been converted into high-end flats. Said, "What's happening?"

"I called the police. I mean, I let her in when she showed me her badge. She had business with the Irish lad who moved in on the top floor. That's what she said, anyway."

"You know him?"

"Who?"

"The Irish lad. On the top floor."

The man shook his head. "Only to speak to. Like, in the stairwell or something. He's not been there long. The girl-friend doesn't like him much... I dunno, you can't judge a person on how they look, right?"

"But she was right," I said.

He said, "I don't know what's happening. This police-woman asking to be let in. Then I heard her banging on the door and then..." He was still crouched, and reached up to tug at my jacket as though to pull me down to his level. "... Jesus, there was gunfire. Gunfire, man!"

"How many shots?"

"I thought you weren't with the police?"

He'd already called them. Which meant I didn't have time to piss around. I said, "How many shots?"

"Just the one."

"Pistol? Shotgun? What kind of weapon?"

"How would I know? I've lived in the Dee all my life. How many guns d'you think I've seen?"

I was tempted to tell him he needed to get out more. Instead, I said, "Stay here. The cops'll be running in like it's Armageddon." Which was true enough. Standard response to a weapons discharge in the city limits was to send all hands to panic stations. They'd be assembling firearms officers, rousing blokes on call from their pits and already someone in PR was preparing press releases to explain the incident. Even though they had no clue as to what was really happening.

I took a deep breath, moved out from behind the car and crossed the road.

Shaking.

Hoping to hell I looked more confident than I felt.

THIRTY-ONE

The first time I met Susan, she had taken me to one side and told me I needed to get in the game. That I needed to put up a mask or just get my act together. Back then we'd been little more than friends. Colleagues who got along well enough. And even so, she'd been a stabilising influence in my life, helped me get ahead.

Until we lost track of the boundaries of our relationship.

When we came back into each other's orbits, almost a year after Elaine's death, she again became a stabilising influence, helping me to process what had happened. She was always in control, always knew what she was doing.

God help anyone who pushed her around.

Which is why I stopped as I walked into Mick the Mick's front room, unable to grasp exactly what it was that I was seeing:

Susan on her knees, her head bowed.

Mick the Mick – a stringy beanpole with greasy hair and an unshaven face that was becoming leathery as he skirted dangerously close to middle age – in front of her, holding a shotgun to her head. "Ya fuckin' bitch. Think if I could kill yer old man, I couldn't kill you?" He looked up, suddenly realising he wasn't alone. "Who the fuck're you?"

"No-one important."

"Then get the fuck out."

"You going to kill her?"

"I've killed before."

"I know. You're a killer for hire, right? Long way from the good old days. Used to be you slung petty drugs. Now you're a real hard man."

He didn't sense the sarcasm. Or he didn't care. "You fuckin' know it."

"Her father, the copper you killed, he was a friend of mine."

"Boo-hoo, buddy. Get the fuck out or I blow her head apart." He jerked the shotgun to make his point, just enough that my eye was drawn to it, not enough that Susan would have a chance to try and take it from him.

Her eyes flicked towards the door. Towards me.

I held my hands out. The kind of gesture you hope is pacifying. "The cops are on their way, Mick. Your pal Wood can't get you out of this one."

"Aye, so she said. I've been inside. I can do the time."

"You killed a cop, Mick. Kill her, you'll have killed two. A two-time cop killer, Mick. Fucking hell, but that's harsh."

He took a deep breath. I had his attention. Hard to tell which way he'd jump. I knew his history, enough about his rep. But what I didn't know was what kind of man he was. Above all, I wasn't a trained negotiator. A lot of cops, of course, receive basic training in crisis negotiation, but the specialists are the ones you hope show up on the scene. Because the basic psychological training most officers receive couldn't help you talk a crisp out of an open bag.

I hadn't exactly been top of the class.

What did the guidelines say? *Allow the suspect to lead the conversation. Personal feelings intrude on the dialogue – never let the suspect know that he's getting to you.*

I'd never handled a situation like this.

"You let her go, Mick, I'll vouch for you. We both will. We'll say that in the end, you did the right thing."

"Fuck you," Mick said. "This pig cunt came to kill me."

I looked at Susan. She didn't move. Her eyes focussed on one single spot on the floor. Absolute concentration.

I took a step forward.

Every step is a victory.

Mick didn't seem to notice.

"They're on their way, Mick," I said. No bluffing. In the distance, coming closer, you could hear the sirens.

Mick said, "I should move fast, then."

Susan moved faster. No warning, no tell-tale tension in her muscles or shifting of her weight. She just brought her hands up, as though in supplication, and grabbed at the barrel of the shotgun, twisting her wrists and her body in opposite directions, so that the barrel pointed away from her. Mick's reaction, jumping back and away from her, helped the process and the barrel swung round and up.

I watched this as though frozen, utterly unable to act.

The flare from the blast as Mick's finger tripped the trigger blinded me. I'd been in the firing line before. The explosion sounded like an old friend. But it was the impact on my shoulder that surprised me. A giant's palm shoving me backwards. At first the pain was surprisingly gentle, more like the sting of a bee than the intrusion of white hot shot slicing through flesh. But as I slammed back against the door frame, the sensation radiated outwards, and increased in intensity. My vision flashed white, as though something had exploded in my skull and started to leak behind my eyeballs.

I blinked, finding myself on my arse, back propped against the doorframe. The pain was an intense and frequent throb that covered my right shoulder and down into the upper right of my chest. I moved my left hand up and felt at the centre of the sensation. My fingers came away sticky with blood and even that small pressure made me want to scream.

I battered my head back against the wall. The impact focussed me. At least for a moment. I looked over to the middle of the room, saw Susan on her feet now with Mick the Mick. The way they moved, the gun held between them, was like a parody of a dance.

Slow. Slow. Quick quick. Slow.

Their edges were indistinct as though their bodies were beginning to melt into each other. My vision was messed up. A word ran through my head: *concussion.*

Fine, I could deal with that.

Had been through worse.

I tried to move. To stand up. But I couldn't. Paralysed. My body just giving up. *No more.*

I had no sensation in my right arm. It was little more than dead weight.

Susan ended the dance. Slammed her knee up between Mick's legs. Sacrificing her balance but giving him something to think about. Her gamble paid off as Mick doubled and let go his grip on the weapon.

She pulled the shotgun from him, swinging as she did so to catch him under the chin with the stock. The blow knocked him back and off his feet. He skited over the bare floorboards and wound up on his back looking up at the woman with murder in her eyes.

She balanced the gun. Both barrels on the Irishman. Said, "One shot left."

Jesus. Didn't feel to me like he'd only fired once.

But did he know that?

Did she?

The sirens outside were quiet. I could hear the scramble of armed response officers outside the flat. Pictured one or two of them grinning beneath their helmets, thinking, *finally, some action.* Some of them had to have been looking forward to an incident like this.

Susan steadied the shotgun.

I tried to move. All I could do was raise my left hand. Slowly. Trembling as I did so like an arthritic old man in his last moments.

I said, "Susan," but it came out like a croak, barely a word. It was enough, though. She turned to look at me. Her eyes catching mine.

Maybe she saw something in there. Maybe she just realised she couldn't do this with someone – anyone – watching.

Or maybe she remembered who she was. All those things she had said to me echoing around inside her head, finally and with a kind of clarity that made her lower the shotgun.

I heard a voice outside the door.

"This is Detective Mollison of Tayside Constabulary… I'm talking to the person…"

Susan yelled back, her voice hoarse and broken, "Hey, Molly! It's Susan Bright. The suspect is… is in my custody."

She let her arms drop, still holding the gun. Turned towards me. She took a step forward. "Steed?"

I tried to smile. Not sure if that only made me look worse. A corpse's grimace.

I heard the flat door open.

Saw a movement behind Susan. But the strength I had found before to move, to make a sound, had vanished. All I could was watch as Mick the Mick scrambled to his feet, shoved Susan in the small of the back and made a grab for that gun.

I heard the stamping of feet from behind me. Voices screaming.

Drop the weapon

Drop the weapon

Drop the fucking gun, you bast –

And then a continuous, mechanical drone that ripped apart the inside of my head and turned my brain to jelly.

I closed my eyes. The sound of automatic gunfire brutally massaged my muscles.

When it stopped, there was a gentle ringing noise some-where in the background of the world.

I thought about opening my eyes. Decided against it. One moment of ignorance.

I needed it. Figured I deserved it, too.

THIRTY-TWO

"You need to take better care of yourself."

I recognised the doctor. Dark hair, tied back. Heavy Mancunian accent. She'd dealt with me when I hurt my hand two years ago. Another gun-related injury. If I wasn't careful, people might start to talk.

I couldn't feel my shoulder. Couldn't tell what was the anaesthetic and what was the damage done to nerve endings by the spread. Shotgun pellets aren't like ordinary bullets. They're filled with shot – tiny, compacted balls of lead – that explode and expand upon release, meaning the closer you are to the weapon the more damage it does. If you're further away, your wounds might not be so bad, but they'll be spread across a wider radius.

I'd been far away from the gun, relatively speaking. The other side of a large living room. Don't know what it was in feet, but whatever, it was far enough that I didn't get my arm blown off or my head knocked off my neck.

So chances were I'd survive. They got to me in time to prevent too much blood loss at any rate. All I could do was hope there was no permanent nerve damage.

I closed my eyes and laid my head back on the pillow. I'd been in enough hospital beds over the last couple of years to know the feel of them, the pillows that felt yielding and yet strangely stiff; just uncomfortable enough to remind you of the clinical nature of the bed you were in.

The tugs and pulls at my shoulder seemed distant and unimportant.

I floated away from them.

Away from the world.

#

"Oy, cuntybaws, wake up!"

I opened my eyes. Lindsay was staring at me from around the same eye level I was lying at. Took me a moment to realise he was in a wheelchair, dressed in the same clinical gown as me. His face seemed hollow and drawn, and the scars were at the stage where they looked a lot worse than you might have expected. There was something of Frankenstein's monster about his post-surgery appearance; as if he was patched together out of awkward-fitting body parts.

I figured I'd keep that thought to myself.

"How long have you been about?" I asked.

"Most of last night and this morning," he said. "They tell me you're more fucked than me." He nodded, sagely. "Good."

I said, "You've talked to Mollison?"

"Oh, aye. He's got some questions for you, lad. You're in for a proper probing."

I hoped he didn't mean literally. "Maybe things are worse than I thought."

"No, this isn't hell," said Lindsay. "Much more shitey than that. This is Dundee." He grinned.

I closed my eyes.

This time, sleep failed to come.

#

When Mollison came to see me, he said, "Every time you're involved in a case, our major suspects seem to wind up dead."

I said, "You can't blame me for Mick."

He shook his head. "What about Wood?"

"What about him?"

Mollison shook his head. "There was a fire at the lockup, McNee."

"What?"

"Big blaze. I'm serious. Would have taken out every storage locker there, maybe the train tracks too, if someone hadn't called it in. Anonymous, of course. As it was, the fire did what I think it was intended to do…"

"…kill Kevin Wood."

"Aye, that's what we thought too. Just as well, too. The prick. See if I'd got my hands on him…"

"Chief Constable's raging?"

"Oh, aye. This bugger climbed right to the top and no-one noticed he was more crooked than any country stile. Of course she's raging."

I said, "But now he's dead, and he can't talk for himself."

"All we have is a paper trail."

"You retrieved Ernie's papers?"

He ignored the question. "And a big mess to clear up."

"Mick was killed by your men."

"Aye."

"By the time that fire was set me and Susan were nowhere near the scene of the –"

"I don't think you set it, McNee. You're a pain in the arse, but I don't think you're a killer."

I nearly asked, *and Susan?* but managed to bite back the question.

Not wanting to answer it myself.

"There'll be an investigation."

"And what about the current investigation into –"

"Officer Bright was lured to the deceased's apartment on the promise of information about the death of her father," said Mollison, the line coming smooth and rehearsed. "Given her emotional state, we do not believe that this relates in any way to her actions of over a year ago which are still being investigated as a separate matter."

I didn't say anything.

"Don't do anything to make us change our minds," Mollison added, not quite as an afterthought.

#

Sleep comes in waves when you're in hospital. Maybe it's the drugs or just something in the air, but the world runs past like a film spliced apart. Time skips. You don't know when you're asleep or when you're awake.

I didn't know Susan had come into the room.

She sat by the bed, watching me until I finally said, "I'm awake."

"How do you feel?"

I considered my answer. Not something I could answer straight away.

In the end I opted for, "Tired," and got the laugh I was looking for.

Susan said, "We need to talk, then."

"Do we?"

She reached out and took my hand.

THIRTY-THREE

The Dundee Herald

TOP COP DRUG "MASTERMIND"

One of Tayside's most senior policeman has been revealed as the "mastermind" behind a country-wide drug trafficking network as well as a series of illegal gambling and loan shark operations.

Kevin Wood, Deputy Chief Constable for Tayside, was exposed by fellow policeman DCI Ernie Bright following a rigorous investigation that ended in tragedy.

Bright, who was murdered, gathered mountains of evidence against his senior colleague with the apparent intent of approaching the Independent Police Complaints Commision with his evidence. Following the Detective Chief Inspector's death, an investigation involving several officers in Tayside CID uncovered the shocking evidence.

DCI Mollison, temporary head of Dundee CID, gave the following statement at a press conference outside Force Headquarters: "We are saddened to learn of the betrayal – not only of the department, but also of the public – by an officer who had been trusted with safeguarding the local community." He went on to add that Tayside Constabulary would be conducting a "housekeeping" exercise to ensure that there were no other links to criminal activity within the force. Three other officers have been identified as working with Wood but their names have yet to be released.

Wood died in a fire at a lockup near Riverside, Dundee before charges could be pressed. The police have yet to issue an official statement on this matter.

#

Ernie's funeral was a sombre affair. Those assembled broke away into small groups following the ceremony. There was an air of hushed uncertainty about proceedings. No-one knew what to say. No-one knew how to deal with the circumstances of his death.

Afterwards, I found Susan at the back of the church, leaning against the stone wall, her head tilted back and her eyes closed. When she realised I was there, she opened her eyes and said, "I can't cry, Steed. I can't cry." Her voice sounded strangled. Panicked.

I stepped forward. She wrapped her arms around me. I pulled her close.

We stood there a long time.

Neither of us cried.

#

I was alone for Mick the Mick's burial. He was interred at the Council's expense, and I was the only person in the graveyard save the Catholic priest, who approached me and said, "You knew the deceased?"

I shook my head.

"Then why are you here?"

"Someone has to be."

He looked at me with his head cocked to one side as though he suspected I had an ulterior motive, one he couldn't quite figure.

I just wanted to see the bastard buried.

When the job was done, I felt some of the feeling come back to my shoulder. As I turned to walk away, rain started to fall from the sky.

#

I waited a couple of weeks before going anywhere near David Burns's house. Even outside, I couldn't be sure why

I was there.

Except I felt I deserved some answers.

He wasn't in.

His wife was the one who answered the door. She stepped back when she saw me, with the kind of look people reserve for the worst kind of devils. The last time I had been at her door was when her husband had gone into hospital after two psycho thugs had tried to kill him.

She still blamed me, I reckoned.

She had to blame someone, even if deep down she knew that her husband brought those evils on himself.

"What do you want?"

"To talk to him."

"About?"

I said, "Fire insurance," and turned to walk away.

She slammed the door.

I knew then that I didn't need an answer. Not really.

The only question I couldn't answer was how he'd known where Wood had been.

And sometimes, you realised that once you know the answer to such questions, there can be no going back.

THIRTY FOUR

Two weeks later.

The sun was out, but the air was brisk. I had to wear a scarf, button up my jacket against the wind.

I stood for a while looking at Ernie's headstone. Thinking how so many people I knew seemed to wind up dead.

But this one wasn't my fault. I had to cling on to that one silver lining.

"I'm sorry," I said, feeling foolish for saying the words out loud. Knowing that if Ernie could see me now he'd probably find the idea of me talking to his grave amusing. He'd have credited me with more common sense than that. "I'm sorry," I said again. "That I doubted you. That I believed the bloody worst of you."

It didn't seem enough.

But it was all I had.

#

After I was done at the graveyard, I drove to the Courthouse, parking two streets away and walking out to the front steps.

I waited there, as I had promised. Not going up. Not going inside.

Susan came out, alone.

She'd been waiting for this day for over a year. The final outcome of the official investigation into her actions during the Mary Furst abduction case. I couldn't tell by her expression what the decision had been. She was composed. Her expression giving nothing away. Even when she looked right at me.

I walked up to her. Said, "Well?"

She took both of my hands in hers and stretched onto her toes to land a light kiss on my lips. It should have been reassuring.

But, really, I couldn't tell.

Notes and Acknowledgements

Yes, it's that time again. You've reached the bit at the back of the book no one really reads except for friends of the author and those looking to try and target contacts in the industry.

It's also worth stating here that *Father Confessor* is obviously a work of fiction. All characters are fictional and any relation to real persons or situations is entirely coincidental. Also, there's no such paper as the *Dundee Herald*. But I think all the pubs are real.

And while we're on the subject, you should note that I don't write these books as a real-life guide to Dundee. Some street names have been made up, moved, changed, mangled or otherwise messed up in the name of dramatic necessity or my own idiocy. You can decide which. However, I do hope I capture something of the city's spirit. I have lived here for twelve years now, and believe that the city is far more interesting and complex than some people give it credit for.

No book is written in isolation. No writer is an island. Many people have had an influence on this book, and below are just a few of the people I'd like to thank this time out.

Mum and Dad: as ever, and for all the right reasons.

Allan Guthrie: Secret Agent Man and Blasted Heathen.

Ross Bradshaw: for pulling out all the unnecessary angst, making the books readable, and not completely killing off Elaine.

Matteo Strukul: who took McNee to Italy.

Robin Crawford, Angie Crawford, Duncan Furness: for last minute interventions, very much appreciated.

The Waterstones Dundee crew: present, past and future – thank you, all!

Booksellers everywhere: too many to mention individually, but your passion, expertise and brilliance are worth a million computer algorithms.

Librarians everywhere: without you, I wouldn't be reading, never mind writing.

The Do Some Damage Crew: for forgiving me the odd slip up on a Friday.

The readers, and everyone who came out to events/signings and talks: without you, there'd be no point.

Alan Bannerman: who will never forgive me for not realising it's a bull.

The usual suspects: Robert MacDuff, Duncan, Gary, Kim, Luke and Ben Smith, Gary and Trish Staerck, Becca Simpson, Jen "The Scientist" McDowall, Karen and Chris Petrie, The Blueshirts and Redshirts, Charlie Stella, Steven Torres, Steve Hockensmith, Linda Landrigan, Christa Faust, Zoe Sharp, Sean Chercover, Tim Stephen, JT Lindroos, Jon, Ruth, Jen and Paul Jordan – for advice, friendship, nitpicking, drinks and a million and one other things that helped get me through. If your name's not there, and you still helped out, know that I'm thinking of you!

Lesley "The Literary Critic" McDowell: for Chinaskis, Paris, New York, Toronto, oceans of wine, and so much more.

In memory: David Thompson (1971–2010)